'My bro... ... a bitter di...

'And what ... ... ate asked.

'It means that my brother has high expectations.' He afforded her a small smile and leaned even closer to her. 'My brother plays games and sometimes he doesn't stick to the rules. He invariably wins.'

'I'm not listening to this—'

'Don't forget, Kate, I'm on your side.'

'Who's taking sides?' she blurted out.

'You will when the time comes. Take care, sweetheart,' he warned. 'Don't play games with my brother. He's off limits to a little gold-digger like you.'

She glared at him. 'If I wasn't employed by the pair of you I'd walk out of here and catch the next flight home!'

'If I didn't need you so badly I'd let you...'

Natalie Fox was born and brought up in London and has a daughter, two sons and two grandchildren. Her husband, Ian, is a retired advertising executive, and they now live in a tiny Welsh village. Natalie is passionate about her cats—two strays brought back from Spain where she lived for five years—and equally passionate about gardening and writing romance. Natalie says she took up writing because she absolutely *hates* going out to work!

Recent titles by the same author:

PASSION WITH INTENT

TORN BY DESIRE

BY
NATALIE FOX

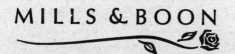

MILLS & BOON

All the characters in this book have no existence outside the imagination of the author, and have no relation whatsoever to anyone bearing the same name or names. They are not even distantly inspired by any individual known or unknown to the author, and all the incidents are pure invention.

*MILLS & BOON and the Rose Device
are trademarks of the publisher.
Harlequin Mills & Boon Limited,
Eton House, 18-24 Paradise Road, Richmond, Surrey TW9 1SR*

© Natalie Fox 1996

ISBN 0 263 79843 7

*Set in Times Roman 11 on 12 pt.
01-9612-52160 C1*

Made and printed in Great Britain

CHAPTER ONE

'GUY LATHAM?' Kate wailed, flicking her shoulder-length auburn bob behind her ears and swinging round from her computer to face Ed Hughes, head of her section.

'I thought that would bring a flush of colour to your cheeks,' Ed drawled knowingly.

Oh, how wrong could he get? If she was sporting a flush it certainly wasn't with fiery anticipation at the mention of Guy Latham. The flush had been brought about by Ed's announcement that she was to fly down to Marbella tonight to help out at the Spanish division of the company. Conrad, the elder of the two Latham brothers who owned the firm, usually handled that end of the commodity-broking company from the Latham villa in Marbella, and twice a year he flew privileged London staff down to familiarise them with what was going on. This time Conrad had picked her so was it any wonder she was glowing? Guy Latham accompanying her on the trip certainly wasn't flush-inducing.

'Th-this isn't a wind-up?' Kate breathed, wide-eyed and scarcely able to believe her good fortune. No, not good fortune. In nine months she'd been a conscientious worker and Conrad, for the second time, was showing his appreciation. The first time, last month, on one of his monthly flying visits to the UK, he had stayed long enough to praise her work to the hilt *and* take her out to dinner. He'd

5

been the most perfect of escorts, a true gentleman in every sense of the word, and by the end of the evening she'd thought she was a little bit in love with him.

'No wind-up, sweetheart. You're definitely booked on a flight tonight.'

Kate was over the moon and her heart was just a little racy. Conrad wanted her and maybe... She gave an inward shiver of anticipation. Conrad was gorgeous. The only black spot on her dizzy horizon was travelling down to Marbella with Conrad's awful brother, Guy 'Lothario' Latham.

If ever there was a man Kate detested it was Guy. If ever there was a man Kate secretly worshipped it was Conrad. A real man. Mature, with taste and sophistication and a solid business head on his broad shoulders. Guy Latham did nothing for Kate's pulse rate, though every female in the company would think her certifiable if she ever admitted it. She had once, though, and learnt her lesson.

'I can't see what you all see in the egotistical creep,' Kate had murmured after one of Guy's morning sweeps through the office. Oh, boy, did he know what he had and how to use it. One steely-eyed look from those piercing dark eyes, the merest hint of a cynical white smile, and anything in a skirt melted at his feet in adoration.

'Huh, you don't fool me, Kate Stephens,' Lorraine Hunter had snapped. 'Why should you be any different? The man is every woman's fantasy hero—tall, dark, drop-dead good-looking, dangerous and desirable. If you can't see that, you must be severely visually impaired. I suppose you think by being standoffish with him he'll want you all the more. Forget it, Guy doesn't bother with challenges.'

Very true. He didn't have to. Women dropped submissive at his feet all the time—and they were welcome. Fortunately Kate had little contact with him anyway but she felt that if she did sparks would fly because one thing about a man she couldn't abide was arrogance and the knowledge that he only had to snap his fingers and some silly female would come running. She was still raw from a previous relationship with someone cast in a similar mould and wasn't looking for further punishment.

No, Guy didn't raise her pulse rate one degree, but—Lorraine adored him and obviously thought Kate was playing hard to get in the hope of snapping him up, and the wrath of Lorraine she could live without. She'd kept her observations to herself after that particular run-in with her.

'And Lorraine is going down with you as well,' Ed added, and came round her console to perch his lean frame on the end of it.

Kate swung back to face her computer and stared gloomily at the screen. That was all she needed. Lorraine was one of that rare breed of women with beauty *and* brains and knew it. For some reason she had never taken to Kate but tolerated her because she couldn't find fault with her work. Kate was good at it and longed for promotion but Lorraine was blocking her way. Lorraine's job of marketing manager was the exalted position Kate would have liked for herself but unless Lorraine left there wasn't much chance. And Lorraine wasn't likely to leave while Guy Latham was still single. Her surname wasn't Hunter for nothing.

'Of course, you know what that means, don't you?' Ed went on, a teasing edge to his tone.

Kate tilted her chin to look at him directly, her dark eyes sparkling, trying to inject genuine interest into them for Ed's sake. He loved a good gossip and that was obviously where all this was leading. 'No, I don't, but I'm sure you're going to tell me,' she trilled.

Oh, how Kate had despised this in-house chit-chat when she had first joined the company, but it seemed to be a way of life to them all. She was used to it now but never partook in it herself, always holding back because she had nothing to offer. She wasn't in the least bit romantically interested in Guy Latham, who to Kate epitomised most men's chauvinistic attitude to women, Conrad an exception, of course.

Ed grinned widely and leaned towards her. 'It means that you haven't much chance with Guy Latham when Lorraine is around,' he said teasingly.

Like I'm interested, Kate thought sarcastically. She gave Ed a disappointed grimace and a slight shrug of her narrow shoulders because that was what he expected. It had never occurred to him that she might be the only woman in the world immune to Guy's dubious charms.

'So they are an item at last, are they?' Kate asked, though it really didn't interest her one little bit.

'Well, his attention to her lately sure looks that way and Lorraine is hardly Miss Innocent,' Ed told her conspiratorially.

Sometimes the men were worse than the women, Ed being a case in point, Kate thought, trying to look interested, her brown eyes still wide with forced curiosity.

'They have had their moments,' Ed went on, 'and it looks like they are in for a few more. Hot, balmy Mediterranean nights and all that. It wouldn't surprise me if they really got it together down there.' He grinned wickedly. 'And you'll be on hand to report back.'

'I'll be on hand to do a job of work, Ed Hughes,' Kate retorted, not able to hide the disgust in her voice this time.

Ed laughed and shifted off her console to pat her head piously. 'Now if that isn't a dead give-away I don't know what is.'

Kate suppressed a sigh of protest. Best not to say anything. No one could ever believe that there was a female in the company who hadn't been bowled over by that dangerous but desirable Guy Latham. Thank God she had never admitted that she admired Conrad more; she'd never have lived it down. Not that Conrad was unattractive—he was better-looking than his younger brother in Kate's eyes. But he was deemed totally unavailable because of serious wealth and seniority and not being around very much, whereas Guy was in the office most days, overseeing the business with steely determination and fluttering female hearts. To Kate he was a bore and a boor.

'So what are my instructions? I'll be flying down tonight, you said . . .'

Kate only half listened to his instructions for her as she gazed past him. It was early August and rain

was shushing against the office window. 'Hot,
balmy Mediterranean nights' evoked thoughts of
love and romance even in a heart as hardened as
Kate's.

Deep inside she longed for love but bitter experience had taught her it was but a dream. She'd
lived that dream with Gustav for a short time then
the nightmare had set in. One woman hadn't been
enough for him but he hadn't had the courage to
tell her to her face; it had been left to friends to
enlighten her, all the more painful to bear because
of bruised pride.

Her mother's attitude hadn't helped. She'd
warned her against him and then hit her with 'I
told you so' when it hadn't worked out. All men
were the same, according to her mother, who had
been cheated on by Kate's father right from the start
of their turbulent marriage.

Kate reluctantly had to agree with her, Guy
Latham being a prime example of everything Kate
was wary of in a man. He was conceited and arrogant and had an ego as whopping as Canary
Wharf, but Conrad was something else—a true
gentleman, a much nicer, gentler man. A *real* man.
Concentrate, Kate warned herself. This was work
and not pleasure. She wanted promotion, didn't
she? It meant more to her than any man ever could
but, on the other hand...*if* she ever fell, Conrad
was certainly in line to be 'fell upon'!

'No, not there, Kate. Behind us. Guy and I have
some things to go over,' Lorraine Hunter
coolly ordered.

Without a word of protest Kate moved to the row behind them in the business-class section of their flight. She was quite surprised that she hadn't been relegated to the back of the aircraft with all the noisy tourists. It was obvious that Lorraine resented her being asked down to Marbella and it was obvious that Guy Latham wondered why she had been picked too.

He had hardly directed a handful of words her way. But that wasn't unusual. Macho man he might be but he had never considered her in line for a conquest so never bothered with her. To him she was part of the office furnishings.

Watching the backs of their heads as the aircraft took off, Lorraine's glossy red-gold, Lothario's glossy blue-black, almost touching as they leaned together to go over some paperwork on their laps, Kate was able to reflect that at least those two were destined for a good time together—but would it last?

Kate supposed she was cynical about the whole concept of love and romance, being an only child from a broken marriage. Her father had eventually left her mother for another woman when Kate was small and she had cut her teeth on her mother's bitterness. But at eighteen she had fallen hopelessly in love with Gustav, in Austria where they had been living at the time. Her mother's predictions had come horribly true and, chastened by the whole painful business of love, she had concentrated on her studies rather than on men.

Conrad was different, though. On landing the job at Latham's Kate had, for the first time in her life, met a man she couldn't help admiring. Here was an older, mature man who could be trusted, the sort who once he fell in love would give his all. Kate closed her eyes and lost herself in a silly, dreamy fantasy to pass the time.

She felt something being eased onto her lap and blinked open her eyes. She glanced down to see the flight magazine and, lying across it, a single red carnation. Her eyes widened and she looked up to see Guy Latham towering over her, all macho arrogance in a lightweight pale grey suit with the sleeves pushed up to the elbows like some stylish movie star. He was smiling, not openly or even in a friendly way—just the small, arrogant smile he used when dealing with the opposite sex.

Kate's stomach tightened and she glanced at Lorraine who was obviously sound asleep with her golden head lolling to one side.

Guy bent down, so close to her that she smelt his cologne. Quite seductively unobtrusive, she noted with surprise. Someone with taste must have bought it for him!

'There's an article in there that might interest you,' he said softly in her ear.

Kate widened her eyes again in surprise. How could he possibly know what might interest her? He didn't know her.

He said nothing more but turned away to speak to the stewardess who had been hovering hopefully and Kate hadn't a chance to flick through the magazine as the seat-belt sign flashed on.

She was still clutching the single red carnation when they landed but quickly discarded it when she realised that it was the one off his meal tray.

The hot Mediterranean air hit them as soon as they disembarked and Kate felt a thrill of excitement. Though it was dark now it somehow added to the buzz of exhilaration inside her. She had travelled widely with her mother, who was a travel writer, and it always excited her.

A chauffeur-driven Mercedes awaited them outside Málaga airport and Lorraine made sure she was squarely seated between her and Guy, which greatly amused Kate. Lorraine just wasn't taking any chances.

'I adore Marbella,' Lorraine enthused as they sped along the busy motorway, west out of Málaga. 'The Spaniards sure know how to live, don't they, Guy? Look at it. Midnight and they are just starting. I could settle here, you know. Sun and the marvellous nightlife...'

She babbled on and Kate closed off, gazing out of the window at the busy hotels, tall palm trees and sparkling lights. She wondered what went on behind the gloss, down the little narrow alleyways with the muddle of whitewashed terraced houses leaning against each other, their tiny balconies dripping geraniums and bougainvillea.

Lorraine nudged her knee. 'You're being spoken to, Kate. Pay attention,' Lorraine seethed.

'Sorry?'

Guy repeated, 'Is it your first time?'

'First time what?' she asked, leaning forward to acknowledge his question. She hoped Lorraine wasn't going to patronise her all the time in front of the Latham brothers. So she was fairly new to the company, but she wasn't a gauche little mouse.

'First time abroad,' Lorraine snapped irritably.

'Hardly', Kate murmured, leaning back in her seat. It struck her that Lorraine was very stiff sitting next to her. She wondered why. 'I went to school in Switzerland and lived in France and Austria for ten years, and when I wasn't studying I travelled with my mother; she writes travel guides,' she told them.

She heard Guy laugh softly.

'Proper little Eurochild, aren't you?' Lorraine said under her breath, and Kate heard another small laugh from Guy.

I'm not going to enjoy this, Kate suddenly thought as they swept off the motorway. Already she could feel Lorraine's animosity towards her. At twenty-two she wasn't a child but if Lorraine kept undermining her this way... But then, when had it been any different since she'd joined the company? Kate was good at her work and for some reason Lorraine resented that, though *her* position in the company hadn't been achieved by her just being a beautiful face. Sometimes Kate didn't understand women, even less so when Lorraine suddenly acted so unsophisticatedly that it almost took Kate's breath away.

'Oh, Guy!' Lorraine breathed ecstatically, leaning across him to gaze out of his side of the car. Security gates had swished open on their approach to the Lathams' villa. 'Have you ever seen anything like that?'

Which was a pretty dumb question, Kate thought, seeing as Guy was part owner of the property. But Kate supposed that she was trying to ingratiate herself with him and acting madly impressed.

So, it was a great-looking place, way over the top for Kate's modest tastes, and she felt a small thrum of disappointment. It screamed out the status of its owners. Kate had honestly believed Conrad to have more conservative taste. It was brashly floodlit for one thing, giving the villa a pinky movie-town glow about it. A Hollywood-style pool surrounded by strident palm trees was the main focal point in front of the villa. The house was sprawling, pink and red-roofed, with an ornate wrought-iron balcony running across the top floor and decorative shutters at the windows. The patios below were of pink-hued marble with reproduction figurines and statues and lush potted plants dotted around. Pillared archways led to the gardens surrounding the secluded property and were floodlit too and promised fragrant walks amongst stunning tropical vegetation—if you could bear the glare of the pink-tinted lighting.

Perhaps it was just fatigue that added to this feeling of disappointment inside Kate at the sight of such gross lavishness. But this was Guy's property too, she reasoned, and flashness was a definite part of his nature, so perhaps it was his taste more than his brother's.

Staff suddenly descended on them from the villa and the disappointment was heightened when Conrad didn't appear and Kate found herself and her bags taken over by a maid who introduced herself as Charo and spoke fairly good English. Charo—pretty, dark-haired and olive-skinned, about the same age as Kate—led her round the side of the villa, away from Guy and Lorraine, who were heading towards the front entrance, Lorraine hanging onto Guy's arm and neither of them even glancing back to see if Kate was following.

'Señor Latham thought you would be more comfortable in the guest house,' Charo told her with a beaming smile.

Kate's heart went into reverse and dejectedly she followed, reminding herself that she was here to work. Lorraine got the main house with Guy and she was consigned to the crummy old guest house, tucked out of the way. And there was she nurturing thoughts that Conrad might have specifically asked for her to be sent over, with amorous intentions in mind. She was more than likely spare to requirements in the London office.

'Oh,' Kate breathed, her hand going to her throat in delicious surprise. Charo had just opened an arched oak door in a white wall and stepped back to let Kate enter. The door opened into a cobble-stoned courtyard—a courtyard so olde-worlde and hot and scented and dripping with grapevines from the dark wooden beams overhead that Kate was overwhelmed. It was lit, but only just. Candles burned in black iron sconces on the rough white walls. 'It's beautiful,' she uttered in surprised awe.

Charo looked happy that she found it so agreeable. 'It's the best part of the estate, the original old *finca*. The rest it came later. Señor Latham love this place. Come inside. I show you.'

Overwhelmed with relief that this was Conrad's personal taste, Kate followed her into the cool, stone-floored house, her heart thudding nervously as Charo showed her round. Conrad had thought she would like this in preference to the opulence of the main house; it was an exciting thought.

It was furnished beautifully with Spanish antiques, nothing over the top. Simple, peasant-type antiques and old Turkish rugs on the polished terracotta floor occupied the spacious main room downstairs. There were several shallow steps and an archway leading to another room. One wall was lined with books, a huge fireplace dominated another, and paintings and small windows adorned another. Upstairs there were three bedrooms, none over-sized. All had old Spanish beds with carved wooden frames and downy mattresses with heavy lace bedspreads. There was matching lace at the open windows. The scent of jasmine perfumed the air from the courtyard below.

The two bathrooms were sympathetic additions to the original rooms, white and gold and cool, and downstairs Charo showed her the small, efficient kitchen that she wasn't expected to use.

'I cook your breakfast and lunch and you dine at the villa in the evening. Señor Latham wanted this part kept away from the main house, so it does not connect. You have to go back the way we came, through the garden.' Charo smiled. 'You like the guest house?'

Kate nodded and smiled happily. 'It's lovely,' she enthused. This was Conrad's taste, not that pretentious villa beyond. And he had allocated it to her. She was overwhelmed with happiness and flattered beyond measure. It was a very special, secret place and already she was in love with it.

'You very lucky,' Charo told her in the main room downstairs as Kate wandered around, smoothing her fingertips over the polished surface of the dark wood dining table. 'Señor Latham allows no one here,' she said meaningfully.

Kate's head shot up and her heart started pounding recklessly as she stared at Charo, whose dark eyes were sparkling mischievously. Charo laughed at her expression. 'I unpack for you.'

'No,' Kate told her quickly with a smile. 'I'd rather do it myself.' She wanted to be alone to take all this in. It was beyond her wildest expectations but a little unnerving. The implications of it all were too much for the moment. 'Thank you, Charo. I'd like to shower and go to bed and—'

'But dinner is being prepared at the villa. My mother, she cooks for everyone.'

'Dinner?' Kate glanced at her watch. She couldn't eat at this time of night, or rather the early hours of the morning. 'No dinner.' She smiled at Charo again. 'Please make my excuses.' Much as she wanted to see Conrad again and to thank him for his thoughtful hospitality, she really was on her last legs.

Half an hour later she was in bed. Cool and relaxed after a long, warm shower. She slept like the proverbial log.

Coffee! She could smell coffee brewing and bacon grilling. Delicious. She stretched luxuriously in the downy bed. Sun filtered dreamily into the room and cicadas serenaded the last remnants of sleep from her muddled head. Charo was cooking her breakfast. I could get used to this, she thought as she yawned and relished another long stretch. But she was here to work.

Reluctantly she got up, washed and dressed quickly in cool white cotton trousers and a canary-yellow camisole top, and, slipping on flip-flops, dashed downstairs. Hopefully Charo would fill her in on the routine here—something Lorraine and the awful Guy had omitted to tell her. She hadn't a clue what time she was expected to start work.

'Charo!' she called. She followed her nose and the aroma of coffee led her out into the shady but still very warm courtyard.

Kate stopped dead in her tracks and let out a small 'Oh' of surprise.

Guy Latham sat at the wooden table under the grapevine, looking coolly elegant in off-white linen trousers and a crisp white shirt, a somewhat surprising multi-hued silk tie at his throat. It was hot—very—but he looked cool, if a little formal for such a climate. His dark hair was slicked back and was still damp from a shower. Kate took all this in because she had time. He was sitting drinking coffee and reading the business section of the *Observer* and might have been in London instead of the jet-set paradise of Marbella.

He looked up, saw her hovering and then glanced back at his paper.

'I don't think you are appropriately dressed for work, do you?' he said without looking at her, as if once was enough.

Oh, first mistake. She should have checked. She felt herself blushing hotly and in confusion went to turn back into the house.

'Hold it! Come back here. Sit down. Charo!' he called out. 'Bring Kate's breakfast and pronto!'

Kate was frozen to the spot now, wondering if he had come to fetch her. Was she late?

He looked up again, sighed in exasperation, folded his paper up neatly and pointed to the wooden chair across the table from him.

Kate crossed the courtyard, sat down and stared at him, feeling a chill of apprehension run through her. She hadn't expected to find him sitting in the courtyard and his abrasive tone was a shock too. Charo put a breakfast plate of bacon, eggs and tomatoes down in front of her and disappeared back into the house. Kate sat mutely and watched him pour coffee for her.

'You haven't been briefed, have you?' he said coldly.

'Briefed?' she uttered weakly.

'Obviously not.' He didn't look very pleased, as if it were her fault.

'Lorraine should have told you,' he said, pushing the coffee-cup towards her. 'Just because the climate is different here it's no excuse for sloppiness. You're late, not appropriately dressed and—'

'Just a minute.' Kate rallied, putting two and two together and coming up with a typical Lorraine put-down. Lorraine hadn't said a word to her about schedules and expectations and that wasn't surprising. Lorraine didn't like her. 'I'm sorry if I'm late, sorry if my attire doesn't meet with your approval, but—'

'Sweetheart, don't give me a hard time,' he interrupted lazily. 'You can come on to me any time in see-through silk and I won't complain but—'

'Don't speak to me that way!' Kate shot back, and was on her feet in a trice, seeing her career slipping away without trace. She wasn't going to be spoken to as if she were another to add to his entourage of adoring women.

'That's what I like,' he drawled. 'A woman with spirit. Sadly it isn't what turns my brother on. Are you getting my drift?'

Wide-eyed, Kate gaped at him. 'No, I'm not getting your drift,' she retorted heatedly, clenching her fists at her sides.

'Sit down, then, and let me tell you about it.'

Sensibly Kate did as she was told, regretting her outburst but only just holding onto her temper.

'Eat before your breakfast gets stale. I'll do the talking and then if you have anything to offer you're welcome to give it a try.' He leaned back in his chair and watched her with dark eyes fringed with thick black lashes.

Kate averted her eyes to the breakfast in front of her. She was starving but couldn't eat, so numb with shock that she couldn't move to pick up the fork. Shakily she managed to reach for the coffee-cup.

'You need more than caffeine to nourish that skinny little body of yours. Now pick up that knife and fork and eat, because if you don't I'm going to have to do it for you and I will,' he threatened darkly.

Kate shot him a look of pure poison. He really was the most arrogant pig she had ever met. He was also one of her bosses. She started to eat.

'That's better.'

Kate gripped her cutlery tightly and glared at him. He might be her boss but she didn't have to take this patronising attitude.

'And that's enough,' she told him firmly. 'I don't like being spoken to in that tone and I don't like being ordered around this way. So I've put my foot in it this morning, but I'm pleading ignorance and I've apologised. I'm not a three-year-old and I'm not stupid. Correct my mistake and give me a dressing down but don't, just don't patronise me.' She started eating and when she looked up at him he was smiling at her—thinly.

'You're executive material, you know.'

'Really,' she mumbled between mouthfuls. Here we go, she thought; he was trying to flatter her now that she had shown a bit of rebellion. She wondered if she was the first to have stood up to him.

'I'm only trying to be helpful,' he said in a softer tone. 'Think yourself lucky you are being addressed by me this morning and not my brother.'

'I'm grateful,' she uttered.

'Sarcasm doesn't become you. Now listen to me, Kate Stephens, and listen good because I'm on your side.'

Kate listened, Oh, yes, she listened, because she knew already that she had overstepped the mark. The trouble was, Guy Latham didn't impress her one bit. She didn't need to kowtow to him because she knew she was good at her job. So she was being a bit risky with him, but she hadn't been asked down here to Marbella for nothing. Only the best got asked and Conrad had put her in his favored guest house and that counted for something. But she mustn't push her luck with his brother all the same.

'Go on,' she murmured compliantly.

'We start work at nine. We dress as we would in an office environment in the UK. The office suite is air-conditioned so you shouldn't suffer any discomfort. My brother expects high standards. This is no different a routine from the usual. We work the same way as we do in the UK.'

Conrad would expect high standards, of course. Kate saw that now and she would respect his wishes because she respected him, though she ruefully thought that a less austere routine would be easier to live with in this heat. Never mind.

'I will deal with Lorraine myself because she should have told you all this,' Guy went on. 'And I'll smooth over your lateness with Conrad and I'll also explain you had a headache or something last night and retired to—'

'What do you mean?'

He eyed her levelly across the table. 'You were expected to dine with us last night and—'

'I wasn't asked!' Kate protested.

'You were *told*. Charo told you.'

Yes, she remembered. Embarrassment engulfed her and she swallowed it down hard 'I . . . I didn't realise and I was tired. I didn't realise I was expected to take my orders from the maid.'

'You take orders from me, Kate,' he told her, scraping his chair back and getting to his feet. His dark, moody eyes met hers. 'Remember that and save yourself unnecessary stress. You answer to me, understand?'

Kate nodded and wished she weren't there. Marbella palled and those hot, balmy Mediterranean nights were but a figment of an over-active imagination. This was all turning into a video nasty, with Guy Latham in the starring role. Poor me, Kate thought as she mumbled, 'I'd better get changed, then.'

'Anything I can do?' he breathed suggestively.

'Yes,' Kate returned defiantly. 'Keep out of my way.'

'And what exactly is that supposed to mean?' he questioned darkly.

Actually she wasn't sure. She supposed it was some sort of warning. After all, he thought himself a gift to women, but surely he wasn't trying it on with her? No, she was sure he wasn't because he'd had nine months to try and not once had he shown her any interest.

'I'm sorry,' she said in response after deciding that a quiet life was very preferable to riling Guy Latham. She didn't want to be thrown off this job before it had even started. 'I'm overreacting. This is my first assignment down here and I'm not at all sure of the procedure. I'll get changed and then perhaps we can start all over again.' She gave him a hesitant smile and he simply nodded.

'I'll wait for you,' was all he said as Kate turned away.

That was something at least, Kate pondered as she hurried upstairs to change into something more businesslike. Lorraine she would tackle later for not preparing her for this. Her reason was obvious. To belittle Kate in the Latham brothers' eyes. Guy, surprisingly, had offered her a helping hand. He probably felt sorry for her. Well, sorry she didn't need from him.

CHAPTER TWO

'KATE. So sorry to hear of your travel sickness. I trust you are feeling better this morning and are eager to get down to some work?' Conrad Latham said formally as he entered the ground-floor office suite attached to the back of the sumptuous villa.

Mind racing, Kate smiled at him hesitantly. Guy had marched her over here without a word, ushered her into a cool, spacious office efficiently equipped with computer consoles and Danish-style furniture—very modern and chic—and left her. Lorraine wasn't around and Kate had stood nervously by the desk at the patio doors overlooking the gardens, just waiting.

So Guy had offered travel sickness as an excuse for her absence at the dinner table last night and her lateness this morning. A lie, which made her wonder at the brothers' relationship. Though they were equal partners it seemed Conrad had the whip hand. Nevertheless Kate was reluctantly grateful to Guy for covering for her, though a little uneasy at the method.

'Yes, I'm feeling much better after a good night's rest, thank you, and—' She was just about to offer further thanks for the lovely accommodation he had put at her disposal when Guy and Lorraine stepped into the room, Guy as steely as usual and Lorraine looking surprisingly pale and disgruntled.

The next few minutes of proposals for the work they were undertaking unfortunately flew over the top of Kate's head as she watched Conrad stride around the room giving out orders. He really was a very impressive man, tall and elegantly dressed in a lightweight grey suit that seemed to highlight the smattering of silver at his temples.

Whereas Guy was deeply tanned, Conrad was quite pale in comparison. Obviously the work-aholic of the two. Kate could imagine Guy topping up that tan by the poolside at every opportunity while his brother wheeled and dealed in this air-conditioned office suite. It endeared him to her even more. She admired a successful man.

'Kate will deal with the German contracts and the redevelopment marketing as she is so efficiently fluent—'

Kate concentrated and glowed inside to think that Conrad thought so much of her, but when the rose mist of adoration cleared from her eyes she realised that it was Guy mouthing the words, not Conrad.

'Lorraine, you are to work closely with Conrad as his personal assistant as you are no good to me on these foreign contracts. Kate is a linguist and of far more use to me—'

Kate felt her stomach somersault in dismay. Lorraine gave her a look as frosty as the Eiger and Conrad simply nodded his acceptance.

'We are restructuring the whole European mar-keting concept,' Guy went on, addressing himself to Kate and Lorraine. 'And I'm afraid the next few weeks are going to be hectic. I apologise for that in advance and my brother and I hope you will bear with us and—'

'Come now, Guy,' Conrad interrupted, giving Kate a look that set her heart pounding. 'Don't expect too much from these beautiful ladies. I'm sure they will benefit from some leisure time while they are with us.'

There was a sudden silence as the brothers caught each other's eye, Guy glowering as if the suggestion should never have been made and Conrad steely-eyed as if exerting some mental power over his younger brother. Guy was the first to concede with a slight shrug.

'Feel free to use the pool and the grounds—strictly out of office hours, of course. This isn't Club Med,' Guy said rather stiffly.

Lorraine let out a small laugh, which didn't surprise Kate one bit. Lorraine would fall helpless at any little joke Guy might attempt. But Kate remained unaffected, seeing the remark for what it was meant to be—a warning, not a joke. It made her wonder what all that had been about this morning—Guy telling her she wasn't suitably dressed, making out that Conrad was the tyrant and expecting high standards. At this moment in time the roles appeared to be reversed, Guy showing far more power and stridency than she had expected in front of his elder brother.

'Kate, you're looking rather pale. Perhaps a tour of the grounds would help you settle,' Conrad suggested kindly.

In utter astonishment Kate widened her deep brown eyes, truly surprised by the suggestion and the implication that he might accompany her. And the way he was looking at her, so invitingly, with smoky grey eyes, made Kate decide that she wasn't mistaken. He *did* mean to accompany her. Her heart fluttered excitedly because on their dinner date his behaviour had been impeccable but now, well, he was sort of flirty, and in front of the others too.

'Kate is perfectly well, Conrad, and there will be plenty of other opportunities to explore the gardens of Babylon, but for the moment work is more important,' Guy stated cuttingly.

Kate's heart began to sink. There was an atmosphere here that made her feel extremely uncomfortable. Power play, and it seemed she was in the line of crossfire between the two brothers. She wished she weren't here.

Before she knew what was happening, Conrad had moved to Lorraine, taken her arm and guided her out of the office without a word from either of them. Kate was left alone with Guy and wishing she weren't because this appeared to be his personal office. She cleared her throat.

'Where do you want me to sit?' she asked in a small voice.

Guy said nothing, indicating a chair at the computer console and walked across the room to the desk by the window, glancing at his watch with a frown and picked up the phone. For a good ten minutes he carried on a conversation in Spanish to a colleague in Madrid, making an arrangement for a meeting in Barcelona and enquiring after the recipient's family, all of which Kate understood, being fluent in Spanish as well. She stared at the dead screen of the computer, waiting for Guy to finish and give her some direction, feeling totally lost and unwanted.

'I apologise for that,' he suddenly said from behind her, so close that she flinched with nerves. 'I had to catch him before he left. Now let's get down to making you feel at home. Conrad was right—you are looking rather pale. I hope I haven't made a mistake by selecting you for this assignment.'

Kate turned her head to look at him, her heart reeling with disappointment, her lips slightly parted with surprise. *He* had chosen her? She didn't understand. She had presumed Conrad... She licked her very dry lips.

'I won't disappoint you,' she mumbled humbly, hating it all, hating him. One small glow inside helped, though, as she thought of the beautiful accommodation Conrad had secured for her. And another glow formed at the consideration he had shown with that suggestion of a tour of the 'gardens of Babylon'—as Guy had so scathingly named the grounds. Conrad was a true gentleman, his brother a heathen. She wished with all her heart that she were in Lorraine's shoes at this moment.

'I doubt you could,' he told her softly, holding her limpid brown eyes with his own. 'But my brother might find you a bitter disappointment,' he added enigmatically.

His hand was on the back of her chair and Kate felt a very small movement, as if he was rubbing his thumb over the back of her white silk shirt. The touch burned and her insides steeled themselves against the intimacy of the touch, but she held it all inside her, glaring at him with a defiance she felt very strongly.

'And what is that supposed to mean?' she asked directly.

'It means that my brother has high expectations.'

'So? I would hope he has,' Kate returned. 'We aren't playing cowboy outfits with your business, are we?'

He afforded her a small smile and leaned even closer to her—so close that she was assailed by that delicious cologne again.

'Indeed not, but my brother plays other sorts of games and sometimes he doesn't stick to the rules. He invariably wins.'

Kate couldn't help the stiffening of her whole body at that innuendo. A warning? That was good coming from him, the Lothario to end all Lotharios. Her contempt for him rose to an all-time high.

'I'm not going to pretend I don't know what you are getting at,' she seethed through tight white lips. 'But I didn't just fall off the olive tree.'

He raised a teasing brow at her. 'Olives are crushed for their virgin oil, dear Kate. Remember that if my brother comes on to you.'

In a fury of shocked embarrassment Kate pushed at the console to free her chair and free herself. She leapt shakily to her feet. Guy had stepped back out of the way of her chair and she swung to face him, eyes blazing.

'How dare you? How dare you speak to me like that?' she cried furiously.

He looked totally unrepentant, even dared to offer her a wicked smile which she was sorely tempted to wipe from his face with the back of her hand.

'Now, I wonder what got your back up? The implication you might be a virgin or that my brother might be toying with the idea of coming on to you?'

Kate opened and shut her mouth in exasperation. Had she heard right? Had this awful, arrogant beast actually uttered those words? I'm going mad, she thought; the heat's getting to me.

'Neither suggestion is worth wasting words on, Mr Guy Latham, but I'm going to do it nevertheless. Both are an insult, to me and your brother. My God, if I was trapped with the pair of you on a desert island surrounded by shark-infested waters I know who I'd turn to.'

'You'd go for a swim, sweetheart,' he mocked. 'Because I'm not to be trusted by implication, my brother's not to be trusted because of fact. Remember that when the heat of the Mediterranean keeps you awake at night.'

'I'm not listening to this—'

He caught her arm as she was about to swing away. He pulled her close to him, knocking the last defiant breath from her lungs. His fingers bit into the soft flesh of her upper arm. He repelled her— so much so that she felt faintness dragging at her.

'Don't forget, Kate, I'm on your side.'

'Who's taking sides?' she blurted out, struggling in his grip.

'You will when the time comes. Take care, sweetheart,' he warned. 'I don't think you fully realise what you have let yourself in for. Don't play games with my brother and don't deny you have something going for him in your heart—'

'I have not!' Kate exploded in defence of her heart and her morality. This was ridiculous; Guy

Latham was as bad as his gossipy staff back in London. OK, so she sometimes toyed with thoughts of Conrad, little fantasies to prove to herself that she was human and needed what all women needed—a bit of warmth in her life. But they were only fantasies. Not once had she ever opened them up to be ridiculed.

'I've known for a long time,' he breathed hard against her. 'I've watched you in the office when my brother's walked in on his monthly calls. I knew for sure when I walked into this room earlier. You couldn't take your eyes off him and I doubt you registered anything that was said. You talk with your eyes, sweetheart, and my brother is a very capable reader. He's off limits to a little gold-digger like you so if I were you I'd cool it.'

He let her go then—so suddenly that her arms fell heavily to her sides. She glared at him, her heart stinging, digesting the warning, fighting him inwardly, deeply shocked that he had put that dreadful interpretation on the interest she had shown in Conrad. He had a nerve. Who the devil did he think she was? Some mindless little tramp who only saw the man's wealth and status? Conrad Latham didn't play games; he was too mature for that. He was a real man and Guy Latham had no right to judge him by his own standards.

'If I wasn't employed by the pair of you I'd walk out of here and catch the next flight home,' she seethed, her eyes bright and warring with his.

'If I didn't need you so badly I'd let you go,' he grated in return. 'And don't get any smart ideas that the feeling is personal. Your bright little brain is needed here and precious little else. Remember that.'

'I don't need any such reminders,' she flamed. She knew she was risking her career by being so outspoken but she wasn't going to allow him to get away with his insults. 'I didn't think for a minute that I was asked down here for decorative purposes and I resent your innuendoes and your warnings and—'

He held his hands up in mock defence and Kate stopped and bit her lower lip. She'd gone too far, way over the top, but he had forced it out of her. She wasn't one of the girls back in London, pandering to his smooth talk, swooning when he walked through the offices. She wanted a career in his company and she was going the wrong way about it by fighting Guy Latham this way. But what price pride?

'Shall we stop this right now before it gets out of hand?' he suggested calmly.

Her eyes fought his for one last time and then her shoulders slumped. She didn't like him but she had to get on with him if they were to work together.

'Yes, yes, we'd better,' she agreed softly.

'Good. Let's put personalities aside and get down to some work.'

He moved away from her and went to his desk and she watched him cautiously. He was still angry, his shoulders stiff and unrelenting. It was odd, but in spite of how she felt about him she had to admit that he was nearly as attractive as his brother. He was thicker set and more sporty and in a few years he'd have the elegance and sophistication of Conrad—if he worked at it.

He turned suddenly and caught her watching him and Kate felt her temperature rise. Heaven forbid that he might guess what she was thinking. She lowered her eyes and sank down into her chair and switched her brain to business mode. That was what she was here for and as far as work was concerned she was determined not to give him reason for more displeasure.

They broke for coffee at eleven, a maid bringing a tray of coffee and small pastries into the office and depositing it on Kate's desk as if she was supposed to serve the lord and master. Kate did, silently, moving across to his desk and putting a cup of coffee down next to him. Lorraine came into the office to break the stillness with her chirpy chatter and Kate left them to go to the toilet.

The modern suite of offices tucked away at the back of the villa intrigued Kate. It was cool and comfortable and the perfect environment to work in away from the heat of the day. She longed for lunchtime, though, so that she could return to that lovely courtyard with its evocative scents and its Andalusian ambience. Already she was seeing it as a sanctuary. A place to gather her thoughts.

Though she had worked hard this morning and tried to block out Guy's awful warnings, they had broken through at intervals. The fact that Guy had noticed the way she had looked at his brother had deeply shocked her. She hadn't realised her feelings had shown. In fact she hadn't realised her feelings were that *strong* to have shown. She respected Conrad enormously and allowed herself a few fluttering fantasies, but was she really looking for love?

'How are you settling?'

Kate swung round in the airy, marble-floored corridor that separated the offices and faced Conrad, her heart fluttering again at his kindly query.

'Just fine.' She smiled shyly. 'You're very well equipped here.'

A dark brow rose with humour at her choice of words and Kate saw the *double entendre* she had unwittingly uttered. She felt the colour rise to her cheeks and it deepened as his smoky grey eyes locked with hers.

'Of course,' he uttered softly. 'I aim to please whenever possible.' The words hung in the air till he added, 'Do feel free to speak up if I can offer you more.'

Kate's insides lurched and Guy's warnings thrummed in her head. But no, she was taking this all the wrong way. Conrad was a gentleman and it was because of Guy's ridiculous suggestions that she was seeing this exchange of words as something it wasn't. Conrad wasn't a flirt. Conrad was simply being the perfect boss and the perfect host as usual.

Kate smiled. 'Everything is lovely. I feel very privileged to be here, Mr Latham—'

'Conrad, please. The environment is very informal here,' he told her with a beguiling smile, teeth as sparklingly perfect as his brother's.

It was Kate's turn to raise a brow. That wasn't what Guy had implied earlier and when she had called him Mr Latham on their dinner date he hadn't insisted on Conrad.

'Conrad, then,' she murmured.

'That's better. Now don't forget, any problems come to me. I want your stay here to be as pleasurable as possible. I'm afraid Guy takes life far too seriously at times. Do you swim, Kate?'

The question took her aback for a second. 'Yes, yes, I do.'

'Splendid. You must join us by the pool this afternoon, during siesta.'

'Thank you; I'd like that.' The thought was already revitalising her stretched nerves. She smiled again and was about to open her mouth to thank him for the guest house when a distant phone ringing diverted Conrad's attention.

'Please excuse me.' He smiled and turned away and Kate nodded.

Her heart was pounding happily and she was stepping on clouds as she went back to her own office. As soon as she opened the door she landed back to earth with a bump. Lorraine had her arms wrapped around Guy and jumped guiltily as Kate entered the room. Guy threw her a dark look which Kate found herself returning with equal black poison. She wouldn't have cared if they had been writhing in passion on the leather couch against the wall, but what stung her was all those warnings he had meted out to her about this being work and not pleasure.

'I beg your pardon,' she uttered, not without sarcasm.

'Knock in future before you come in, Kate,' Lorraine scythed at her, and straightening her lace-edged top over her narrow pencil skirt, she strode towards the door Kate had left ajar. 'I'll be ready at two, Guy.' The door slammed after her.

Kate sat at her console, punched the keyboard viciously and stared obliquely at the screen.

'Yes, knock before coming in, Kate,' Guy repeated into the uncomfortable stillness that had enveloped the room after Lorraine's brittle exit.

Kate held her lips tightly clamped. She wasn't going to say one word and she didn't.

They broke for lunch and siesta at one o'clock, Guy reminding her to be back on duty at four-thirty before leaving the room. Kate nearly stuck her tongue out at the back of the door but resisted the temptation for fear of Guy poking his face round the door and catching her. He already thought her . . .

What exactly did he think of her? she wondered as she left the office suite, the hot Mediterranean air hitting her, in sharp contrast to the cool of the air-conditioned office. He thought she had a good brain for one thing; not much else, though. Oh, she'd forgotten, a gold-digger. Huh! She should care.

The perfumed courtyard was a welcome refuge. After the morning's idiosyncrasies she couldn't face a swim, even with the thought of joining the man she so admired. She understood why everyone broke off for a siesta in the afternoon; fatigue was dragging at her very bones.

'Charo?' she called out as she stepped into the coolness of the stone-floored guest house.

Silence. Kate was relieved. She didn't want to talk or even breathe in this heat. Her head was enough to cope with. She changed into a cool sarong over her lacy underwear, made herself a coffee and cut a chunk of crispy bread and a slice of goat's cheese, sat in the shade of the vines to eat it, and then shifted to the tiny garden that led off an archway from the courtyard.

'Heaven,' she breathed as she collapsed into a cushioned cane lounger under a knobbly old olive tree. Her eyes were heavy as she gazed up at the clumps of fat green olives amidst the spiky silvery leaves. Virgin oil, she mused, and it was her last thought.

'You idiot!'

Kate woke with a start, blinked fearfully and tried to sit up. She was alone and yet she could have sworn someone had shouted her awake.

'Oh, no!' she breathed in agony, and gazed down at her left leg. Her sarong was gaping open, right up to her thigh, and the whole of one long, shapely leg was exposed to the punishing rays of the sun. The top of her leg was worse than the rest, the more tender skin red with inflammation.

'Stay still,' Guy Latham growled as he came through the archway to the secret garden, his hands full of stiff, spiky green ... *cactus*?

Kate squealed in alarm as Guy came towards her with them.

'What the hell—?'

'Yes, well you might cry hell, sweetheart,' he growled again as he dropped the spikes at her feet and in one deft movement hauled her, in the chair, further under the shade of the olive tree. 'Don't you know never to sunbathe at this time of day in Andalusia?'

'I wasn't sunbathing,' Kate defended herself angrily, and then winced painfully as she tried to move her stiffened leg. It felt as if her skin had shrunk and was too small for her bones. 'I ... I must have fallen asleep. The sun moved,' she bleated weakly.

'Well, it does that,' he grated sarcastically, and proceeded to split open the succulent, spiny leaves he had brought with him.

'What on earth are you doing with those?' she cried, shrinking away from him.

He sat on the edge of the lounger and grasped her ankle firmly with one hand and with the other scooped out a pale jelly-like substance from the insides of the spines.

'No!' Kate cried, and then instantly let out a small cry of relief as he slapped the cooling jelly over the worst of her raw thigh. 'Oh, I don't believe it!' she gasped, and slumped back against the lounger and sighed deeply. It was bliss, sheer heaven as he gently patted the jelly over her fiery skin to cool it.

She opened her eyes when the crisis was over and stared at his fingers as they smoothed over her thigh. Then she was in crisis again as one delicious sensation moved over for another. His touch was so sensuous—astonishing, coming from him. Her whole body tensed and she wanted him to stop but he wasn't about to. More cooling jelly was applied till she thought she couldn't stand the wondrous feeling a second longer. She tried to pull her leg back out of his reach but he held onto her ankle firmly.

'Keep still,' he ordered quietly.

Kate said a silent prayer of thanks that it was only her thigh that was affected. Supposing it was her chest that had been so painfully exposed to the sun's rays? A hot flush engulfed her and she let out a small cry at the thought. What on earth was happening to her?

'Don't,' she pleaded weakly. 'That's enough.'

'Let me be the judge of that,' he uttered under his breath.

There was a sliver of stinging skin on her inner thigh that had caught the sun as well, and he turned her ankle to gain access to it.

Kate pulled away, shrank back from him, her eyes wide with terror, her heart nearly seizing. Guy held on more firmly. He looked up to catch the panic in her eyes. He frowned.

'I wonder if you would be quite so reticent with my brother if it was he tending your sunburn?'

Kate kicked out at that nasty suggestion, jerked her legs so sharply that the pain shot through the whole of her body.

'Stop being so touchy and keep still. I'm doing this for your benefit, not mine,' he growled.

'Huh,' she huffed angrily. 'I wasn't suggesting you were getting anything out of it for yourself, though you're certainly taking your time about it! Give it to me!' She snatched at the thick succulent and instantly cried out again as one of the sharp spines dug into her thumb. 'Ouch!'

Guy tutted impatiently and grabbed at her hand. To Kate's complete horror he stuck her thumb in his mouth and sucked at it. Eyes so wide that they hurt, Kate watched as he drew sensuously on her thumb, tenderly running his tongue over the spot the spine had jabbed. His eyes, hooded and oh, so dark, held hers as he did it.

Kate gasped with the shock of what he was doing and the way it was affecting her. Her insides twisted alarmingly. She wrenched her thumb, her thigh, her whole being out of his reach. She was on her feet in a trice, pain shooting down her leg at the sudden movement and rocking her with the horror of it all.

'What are you, for heaven's sake—some blood-starved vampire?' she screeched.

She didn't wait for an answer but hobbled painfully out of the garden, through the courtyard and into the house. She stood trembling at the kitchen sink, running the cold-water tap and trying in vain to catch her ragged breath. She felt sick, horribly so. She fought it, though, because she didn't want to embarrass herself even more by fainting or actually being sick in front of him. Oh, misery. Why had she fallen asleep so carelessly?

She heard movement behind her, bottles in the fridge clinking.

'Don't drink the tap water; here—take this.'

She swung angrily to face him, afraid she was going to burst into tears. Her thigh ached miserably, her thumb stung, her head was about to split and she was going to be sick. She grasped at the tumbler of bottled water he held out for her and drank thirstily. It was just what she needed to bring her equilibrium back.

She sank the empty glass into the sink. 'Anything else?' she questioned fiercely. 'It seems when you are around I can do nothing right!'

He looked at her and shrugged. 'Your personal life does have a knack of going awry when I'm not around.'

'You think!' she retorted.

'I *know*,' he responded firmly. 'You need wet-nursing.'

'I need nothing of the sort. So I've made a few mistakes—missed dinner, overslept, dressed inappropriately, looked at your brother the wrong way, fallen asleep in the sun—crumbs, none of them certifiable!'

'So why are you making so much fuss about them?'

'I'm not! You are the one . . . the one . . .'

'The one what?'

All the breath went from her then and she lifted her trembling fingers to knead her hot brow. What was happening here? He threw her all the time. Made her feel gauche and so terribly out of it. This assignment was going all wrong and he was at the root of it all.

'I'm going up to shower,' she uttered helplessly, and went to turn away.

He caught her arm and spun her back to face him.

'No, you're not, sweetheart. You haven't time. Another *faux pas*. It's nearly four-thirty and you only have time to get out of that scrap of cotton and into something decent before you are back on the job. Standards and all that,' he mocked.

Wide-eyed, Kate glared at him. She couldn't win with him whatever she did. Her eyes dropped contemptuously to his fingers gripping her wrist and then she gasped in horror.

'I'm bleeding!' There was blood on her arm where he was holding it.

He looked down and as he let her go he said impatiently, 'You're not but I am.'

He held his hand up and Kate was filled with remorse when she saw where the flow of blood was coming from. The tips of his fingers were cut where he had ripped open the spiny cactus leaves. Her sun-scorched thigh didn't sting any more because of his quick, healing treatment. He hadn't given a thought to himself, just torn those leaves apart to relieve her pain.

Without further thought she took his hand and thrust it under the still dribbling tap.

'Who needs wet-nursing now?' she breathed.

'This is turning into a real kitchen-sink drama,' he said as she held his fingers under the cooling water.

For the very first time in nine months Kate smiled at him. He was quite amusing when he dropped his arrogance.

'What was that stuff anyway?' she asked as she dabbed at his fingers with a piece of clean kitchen roll.

'Aloe. Nature's way of compensating. A natural balm for sunburn growing where it is needed. Isn't life wonderful?'

He held her eyes with his. They were dark and smouldering and provoked another first for Kate: she could almost see what all the females in London saw in him. He had a certain *je ne sais quoi*. But she wasn't prone to falling for indefinable somethings.

She let go of his hand and smiled at him sweetly. 'Yes, bloody amazing,' she retorted, and left him to make the best of his injuries by himself.

CHAPTER THREE

DINING at the villa that evening was going exactly the way Kate had thought it would—disappointingly. Not that she had been brimming with expectations, because, thanks to Guy Latham, the whole assignment wasn't proving to be a privilege as she had anticipated but more a slow death by underprivilege. She felt thoroughly put down by Lorraine's appearance, in flowing, silver-threaded chiffon with sparkly bits around the plunging neckline. In comparison Kate felt dowdy in her mink-coloured silk dress bought in last year's sales.

She sat stiffly across from Lorraine at the long, polished Spanish oak table on the front terrace of the villa. The Hollywood-style pool glittered beyond the white stone balustrade, blue and inviting, promising to balm this awful throbbing thigh of hers if she dared to take a plunge in it, which she so longed to do. It would certainly liven up the evening if she did strip off and take a sprint for it!

Kate wondered where Lorraine and Guy had gone during the afternoon, because for sure Lorraine hadn't been exposed to the sun. She was as pale as ever, perhaps a little more so than usual. On returning to the office after siesta Kate had found herself ensconced with Guy in their office and she hadn't seen any sign of Lorraine, or Conrad, come to that, till now.

Conrad looked wonderful in a white evening jacket and narrow black trousers. Kate reluctantly conceded that Guy didn't look bad in similar attire either. The brothers sat at either end of the long table and intimate conversation, because of the distance, was difficult.

Kate's heart flipped as Conrad's voice boomed over the buzz of cicadas in the heavy, hot night air.

'Kate, I'm disappointed you didn't join me for that swim as you promised. I was looking forward to it.'

Lorraine glowered at her as she forked prawns between her pink lips. Kate *felt* Guy glowering at her but she couldn't look at him; to do that and converse with Conrad she would have had to turn her head this way and that as if she were at a tennis match.

'Kate is still acclimatising to the change of temperature, Conrad,' Guy answered for her. 'If you spent more time in miserable, wet London you might be able to understand why.'

Conrad laughed and Kate squirmed, hoping she might be wrong in thinking that there was a barb under Guy's remark. It obviously hadn't registered with Conrad.

'I'm sure Kate is quite able to answer for herself, Guy,' Conrad offered drily, the laughter short-lived.

Oh, yes, it had registered!

Because of the aloe, and only because of the aloe, Kate spoke up. 'Guy is right,' she directed at Conrad. 'I think my biorhythms are out of sync. I fell asleep this afternoon and didn't wake up till ... till it was time for work again.' Her thigh stung as a reminder of exactly how she had woken up. She wasn't about to mention it, though. Lorraine would love it—sunburn on her first day here.

'You're driving her too hard, Guy. Ease up a bit.'

'If I eased up this business would grind to a halt,' Guy said, and Kate wondered if anyone but her had heard.

'And you, dear Lorraine. What kept you out of the pool today? How you girls have disappointed me.'

So, Conrad had invited Lorraine too. Kate felt a small frisson of disappointment.

'Guy was kind enough to offer to drive me down to Puerto Banus, Conrad. My cousin is thinking of investing in a time-share apartment overlooking the marina and I wanted to check it out for him.'

'Time-share never was a good business investment,' Guy commented. 'The market is saturated with unsold properties.'

'I'll take your advice on that, Guy, darling,' Lorraine enthused, giving him an adoring smile. 'I'm sure you know best being so familiar with the area. And you, Kate—what would your advice be on investing in a time-share? Surely you have a viewpoint?'

Kate knew instinctively that Lorraine was putting her on the spot, probably sensing that she knew absolutely nothing about the subject. She was right—she didn't; she only knew that several people bought a certain number of weeks each of the same property.

'I'd say if you were the developer you were onto a smart little earner if you managed to sell all the weeks. As a buyer I wouldn't consider it. I shudder at the thought of sharing the same bed as all those strangers!'

There was an explosion of laughter from each end of the table, with Conrad slapping the polished surface with a resounding thud that momentarily stilled the cicadas.

'Nice one, Kate,' Guy offered, still laughing as he stabbed at his prawns.

Kate ventured a glance at a po-faced Lorraine sitting across from her. If looks could kill . . .

Later, Kate excused herself after the brandies were served further along the terrace. Lorraine sat heavy-lidded in one of the flamboyant peacock cane chairs. Tomorrow Kate would advise her that a siesta was advisable in this climate—but then again she might not. Lorraine could find out the hard way, as she had left Kate to find out everything about this trip the hard way. Clothes for one thing. Lorraine might have advised Kate to bring more dressy wear for the evenings. She definitely felt underdressed. She'd heard that shopping in Puerto Banus was a treat; perhaps she could hire a car and get out for a few hours and buy some new clothes.

'Goodnight, Kate,' Conrad said politely, rising from his chair to lay a hand lightly on her shoulder. 'Perhaps tomorrow your biorhythms will be balanced enough for you to join us for a swim.'

'Hopefully, yes.' She smiled and bid everyone goodnight, including a bright Lorraine, who had certainly perked up as Kate was preparing to leave.

'Don't bother waiting up for him,' Lorraine said under her breath as Kate reached down for her evening bag by her chair. 'He'll be very late—if he turns up at all.'

That one was definitely beyond Kate but perhaps Lorraine had over-indulged in the brandy; she'd certainly gulped it down as if a hangover wasn't a consideration.

Kate took the long way round the villa to the lovely old guest house. She wasn't a bit tired, just bored with the conversation at the dinner table. Just as Conrad was about to strike at an interesting subject Guy always seemed to knock him back and Lorraine had very little to offer in the way of scintillating conversation apart from office gossip, which seemed to be a million miles away at the moment. Kate was beginning to wonder where she had got the idea that the lovely girl had a brain.

Nothing was going the way Kate had expected. She supposed she had expected too much, seeing this trip leading to some sort of promotion for her. She loved the company and the dealings she had with overseas traders and she wanted her own department, but this trip so far was having a knock-back effect on her. It was all a bitter disappointment—all except Conrad. He was as charming as ever, if not more charming than ever.

Kate breathed the heavily scented night air and wandered through the floodlit gardens, admiring the lush greenery of feathery ferns and the colourful, droopy hibiscus flowers. She thought that sprinklers must be on all day to keep the foliage so lush.

''Ello, Vera,' she whispered, and bent to flick at the thick, spiny leaves of the plant Guy had used to soothe her sunburn.

'Very amusing.'

Kate jumped and spun round to face Guy. Why did he always catch her unawares and make her feel so small?

'Talking to the plants, eh?'

'Better folk than me do it,' she told him, lifting her chin and carrying on strolling down the winding path that she hoped led to the back of the guest house. If she got it wrong and ended up in the compost, he'd be there like the ubiquitous empty Coke can lurking in the corner.

'Are you tipsy?' he asked, striding along beside her, hands plunged casually into his trouser pockets, straining the fabric across his . . . hips.

'You don't have to be legless to talk to the pants— plants,' she corrected herself quickly. Perhaps she had over-indulged a bit in the oaky red wine they had drunk with the steaks and that lovely smooth brandy with the coffee, but that was under-standable, given the circumstances of extreme boredom.

He gently took her elbow. 'Come, let me make sure you get back safely.'

She jerked her elbow out of his reach. 'I'm not, you know.'

'Not what—a virgin?'

'One-track mind,' she said drily. 'I'm *not* tipsy.'

'Perhaps just a little mellow around the edges, then.'

'Yes, perhaps,' she conceded with a small murmur.

'Talking of tracks, this way, not that. To your rescue once more, don't you think?'

He took her elbow again, directed her to the left, not the right where she was veering, and she let him because she had allowed a small fantasy to replace his bulky frame next to her; she had replaced him with the image of his gentlemanly brother escorting her through the scented gardens.

She imagined his arm going around her shoulder—a good, strong masculine arm that would keep her safe. She imagined him unobtrusively drawing her head to his shoulder. She imagined him slowing his pace in a shady part of the foliage where the scent of jasmine made the senses swim. She imagined him turning her face to his and slowly, oh, so slowly and sensuously, brushing his lips across hers.

But there was something wrong and in her head she struggled to get the images right. Conrad's face didn't fit and . . . and she was glad. She didn't want Conrad's lips on hers. She wanted Guy's, and she was confused, but the confusion didn't matter.

Guy's lips captured hers and the feeling was wondrous. His mouth on hers. A kiss so deep and caring and safe and mature. A kiss with a promise of true feeling, a promise that it wouldn't be the last, a promise that at last he had found a lover worthy of his sophistication.

Deeper and deeper she sank as his arms held her so strongly. The kiss swelled her heart till she swayed dizzily. She felt floaty, as if carried away on a puffy cloud of sensuality.

She drew back slightly, not wanting it to end but wanting to breathe his name sensuously, to let it hang like a drifting, moon-silvered cobweb over their heads and to show in the depths of that small utterance that she cared.

'Guy!' she screeched. Her whole body stiffened with horror as her eyes blinked open and focused on the face in front of her and she realised what she was doing: kissing the enemy.

He let her go as if he had been shot at close range.

'What the—?'

'How...how dare you do that to me?' Kate croaked, grasping at her throat as if he had half strangled her. Embarrassment then momentarily flooded the attack from her. For a second she wasn't sure who had done the running just now— but attack was the best defence, surely?

'How dare *you*?' he flamed.

She could just see the dark anger in his eyes and the injustice of it fired rage through her. 'Me?' she squealed.

'Yes, you. Coming on to me and then throwing hysterics. I might have known—'

'*I* might have known!' she blurted out hotly, her whole body burning at what had just happened. 'You can't let one single female in your life go un-challenged, can you?'

'Unchallenged!' he scathed. 'I put my arm around your shoulder to guide you and the next moment you were in my arms and—'

'No, way, José!' she cried defensively. 'I'm not taking that! You're nothing but a scheming op-portunist. Oh, how dare you? Why, I...I...'

'Enjoyed it?' he suggested daringly, all anger gone now, a smirk on the lips that had just plun-dered hers so deeply.

'Enjoyed it?' she echoed incredulously, writhing inside at the very thought that he might think that. 'I'd rather kiss the blunt end of a...of a donkey than you!'

'Charming,' he uttered teasingly, hands plunged back in his trouser pockets again.

'Well, charming you are not, Guy Latham, and gullible I am not. One drippy, love-struck female on this assignment should be enough for you. I'm not prepared to feed your swollen ego by falling rapt at your feet. If you...think....' Her voice trailed away, fading as she realised she was putting up some fight here—a fight that might be misinterpreted as a...a challenge. 'Struth! If he shared the thought that Lorraine had once put to her—that by being standoffish with him...

Cold shudders ran through her, calming her, sobering her. Her back stiffened rebelliously.

'Thank you for heading me in the right direction,' she told him primly, chin raised. 'I'll find the rest of the way myself.'

He smiled, oh, so damned knowingly, and then he nodded to behind her and she swung round to see the arched wooden door that led to the sanctuary of the scented courtyard. She turned her head and gave him one last black look of defiance which he acknowledged with a very slight nod and then she was through the door, slamming it shut behind her and leaning back against it, taking ragged hot breaths into her lungs.

'Sweet dreams, sunshine,' he called out over the white wall.

In a rage of embarrassment Kate bit at her white knuckles to stop herself wailing. How could she have allowed that to happen? She didn't like him! She didn't! She didn't and yet . . .

Covering her face with her hands, she held her breath, listening for the sounds of his receding footsteps. With relief she heard them, and something else. Was he whistling softly to himself? Oh, how she hated men who whistled. Oh, how she hated Guy Latham, and how on earth was she going to face him tomorrow across that cool, cool office? She dreaded the thought.

Kate had had a rotten night. She awoke with a headache and her first thought was for Lorraine, who must have a belter of one, considering the amount she had consumed the night before. Kate *hadn't* been tipsy, but there again she must have been to have actually enjoyed that kiss . . . No, she hadn't enjoyed it and . . . and Guy . . . No, no, no!

Oh, her head wasn't her own and she wondered if the cloying heat had something to do with her feeling so muggy and confused this morning. And what on earth was wrong with Spanish plumbing? She'd heard water running in the night and funny sounds as if someone had been moving around along the landing.

She stretched and glanced at her watch on the cane bedside table. At least she had woken early enough not to be late. She could afford another five minutes to allow her head to steady but decided against it. Better safe than sorry. If she fell asleep again and *was* late Guy Latham would just love it.

She showered, washed her hair, blow-dried it into a glossy bob and dressed. In another few days she'd ask if she could have a few hours off for some shopping. She hadn't expected to have to make do with the two shirts and two skirts she had brought with her. The rest of her stuff was very casual—too casual for Guy Latham's stringent standards. Oh, hell, why should she care what he thought?

She let out a silent groan of misery as she stepped out into the shady courtyard. Her tormentor was sitting in the same place as yesterday morning, drinking coffee and perusing the paper—*El País*, the Spanish daily, this morning.

She sat across from him and heard Charo moving around in the kitchen.

'This isn't necessary, you know. I only have to be told once. I've learnt my lesson and I promise not to be late again and it really isn't necessary for you to come here and frogmarch me to my duties every morning. Yes, coffee, please, Charo.' She acknowledged Charo's waving coffee-pot mime from the doorway of the old house. 'Not a cooked breakfast, though. Have you any rolls, please?'

'Continental breakfast, *sí*.' Charo laughed. 'You learn quickly, Señorita Kate. You mad English with your bacon and eggs in this heat.'

Kate gave her attention back to Guy who as yet hadn't given her his.

'Did you hear what I said?'

He folded the paper and put it down on the table. 'Every delightful word that tripped off your sweet lips,' he murmured sarcastically.

'I have learnt my lesson, you know. See, I'm early this morning, and please don't feel obliged to—'

'Frogmarch you to your duties,' he echoed wearily.

'So you were listening.'

'Indeed I was.'

'Coffee, rolls, *señorita*,' Charo sparkled efficiently.

'*Gracias*, Charo.'

The maid laughed. 'You speak *español*?'

'*Bastante*.' Kate smiled back.

Charo laughed. 'Enough, *sí*. You excuse me, then, if I speak my tongue to Señor Latham.'

She proceeded to rattle off in Spanish to Guy and as Kate listened she poured her own coffee... right over the edge of the cup! Shakily she put the heavy pot down with a thump and stared incredulously at Guy across the table. He was listening intently to Charo's enquiry of concern but watching Kate at the same time.

Then he was apologizing and telling Charo it was nothing and that he was perfectly all right and he was sorry for giving her extra work, and yes, would she be so kind as to oversee the work that needed to be done in the second bathroom as he was too busy, and yes, he trusted her judgement to make sure her cousin did the work to his usual high standard and... and no, it was no inconvenience to share his guest's bathroom while the work was being carried out.

Charo, satisfied, went back, grinning, into the house. Kate sat rigid and uncomprehending, only her fingers stiffly working with her napkin to mop up the coffee she had spilt.

'Did you understand all that?' he asked.

Her head buzzed and she nodded and swallowed to allow herself to speak. 'I learnt my Spanish from a Catalan who didn't drop his s's as the Andalusians do, but I understood most of it.' Her eyes went to his fingers, which were still very red.

He wiggled them to show all was well. 'Charo worries about me,' he told her. 'She panicked when she found blood on my towels.'

'The . . . the towels in your bathroom,' she said in a small voice. She'd had no idea, none whatsoever.

'I hope you don't object to sharing your bathroom with me while the plumbing in my bathroom is being repaired?'

She couldn't raise her eyes to his. She concentrated on ripping her crusty roll to small pieces and smothering them with strawberry jam. This was *his* house and he was in residence and she hadn't known. She felt a small amount of anger at being fooled, but then he hadn't exactly fooled her, just omitted to tell her, and she, like a dizzy idiot, had presumed that Conrad had set all this up for her.

Thank goodness she hadn't made a further fool of herself by expressing her grateful thanks to Conrad for his kind consideration. If there was any thanking to be done it should go in Guy's direction. But she wasn't about to humble herself to him, certainly not after what had happened last night.

'What's wrong? You look as if you've seen a ghost.' He topped her coffee up for her and she raised her dark lashes at last and looked at him.

'I didn't know,' she offered weakly.

'Didn't know what?'

She sighed in exasperation. 'I didn't know I was sharing this house with you,' she said more strongly. She felt more anger tingling at her spine now but wondered at it. Maybe she was cross with herself for being so naïve, actually believing that Conrad thought so much of her that he had allocated this lovely old house to her. So why had Guy?

She asked, 'So why am I here and not Lorraine? I would have thought this place was ripe for seduction!' Oh, God, she wanted to bite her tongue for letting that slip out.

'Seduction, eh? Is that how this lovely place strikes you—a site suitable for seduction?'

'Of course not,' she snapped hotly, and popped a piece of roll into her mouth. She chewed on it and he watched her, unnerving her even more by leaning across the table to get closer. She saw the look of mockery in his eyes; he knew he had her in a spot and, yes, was loving it.

She swallowed hard. 'The environment doesn't matter. I mentioned seduction because that is what screams out from the pair of you. You and Lorraine, an item. You can't even keep your hands off each other in the office.'

'Correction. She can't keep her hands off me. But that is beside the point.'

'It *is* the point,' Kate emphasised. 'I don't see why she's over there in Caesar's palace and you're over here in the *campo*. A bit odd, that. This isn't your style, I would have thought.'

'You know nothing about my "style" and even less about the relationship between me and Lorraine. I'd tread very carefully if I were you. You just might stomp your clumsy way over some very delicate emotions here.'

He was right—seduction was a very delicate subject if you were involved in it. This was none of her business.

She sighed and carried on eating her roll and sipping her coffee. Now she understood the meaning of what Lorraine had murmured to her last night. Lorraine knew, obviously Conrad knew—the whole world but her had known that she was sharing the same roof with the awful Guy Latham. And now she was going to have to share the damned bathroom with him too.

So now she knew but what she still didn't understand was why she was here and not Lorraine. Perhaps she had got it all wrong and this lovely old house wasn't the bee's knees, as she saw it, but in fact second-class accommodation for a lowly, second-class employee, and Guy was simply here to make sure she didn't run off with the silver!

'You still haven't answered my question—why you saw fit to put me in here.' And why was he staying here when the flamboyant villa was so much more in tune with his character?

'The truth?' he murmured, leaning back and stretching his arms above his head.

'Of course the truth!'

He could be so exasperating. Mocking, teasing, unpredictable. How could any woman fancy him when he was so *annoying*? Oh, no, there went her heart again, flipping and flopping like her flip-flops.

He folded his arms across his chest after his long, lazy stretch—those tanned, sun-tipped, hair-covered arms that had wrapped around her last night. She hadn't been the one to make the first move . . . OK, OK, perhaps she had, but she had been possessed, surely? And he must have known that but he sure hadn't put up a fight. The creep.

'I thought you might appreciate a piece of old Spain, but it's obvious I made a mistake. It's clear you feel put out by not being housed in Caesar's palace—'

'Just a minute. I said nothing of the sort . . . well, I know I called it Caesar's palace but I didn't mean it the way you took it. I mean . . . I meant . . .' She was fumbling and they both knew it.

His eyes held hers, mocking her again.

'You spoke of *this* place as the *campo*—'

'I didn't mean it the way it came out . . . in a derogatory sense. I meant it in the Spanish way—you know, the countryside. Charo told me it was the original old *finca* on the estate before—'

'Before my brother ruined it?' he finished for her in the style of a question.

She squirmed inside. 'I didn't say that either.'

'So you admire my brother's architectural bad taste?'

Kate stared at him hard. *Conrad* was responsible for the garish villa? She could hardly believe that! And she could hardly believe that Guy recognised the villa as bad taste.

'Where is all this leading?' she asked in a small voice.

Guy shrugged. 'Nowhere, I suppose. I just wanted to satisfy myself that I hadn't made a mistake in my character judgement of you.'

'Have you made a mistake?' she bravely asked.

'I don't know because you have the knack of squirming your way out of any direction in our conversations. I thought I might get to know you

better by bringing you down here but you are
making it hard going. Always on the defensive,
always putting the barriers up.'

Kate refused to let any of that get to her. He
thought he might get to know her better . . . it didn't
bear thinking about. She let out a small laugh.
'Familiarity breeds contempt, Guy Latham. I work
for you, don't forget.'

'And yet you speak to me at times as if the boot
is on the other foot.'

Kate reached for more coffee. The pot was out
of her reach so he lifted it for her and topped up
both their cups. She was extremely uncomfortable
now, knowing she had gone far too far with him
since they had arrived here.

'It's different here,' she told him quietly.

'Go on,' he urged, leaning back to drink his
coffee.

She had been pretty blunt with him since coming
here so there was no reason to be coy now.

'It's different here because . . . well, I've had no
reason to have much contact with you before. In
London I go to Ed Hughes with my problems. I
know you are my boss and I realise that I've
probably gone over the top with you in the way I've
spoken to you, but that's your fault.'

'How do you make that out?'

She shrugged. 'Your attitude, I suppose, and
your reputation as some sort of dangerous heartbreaker. Apparently women go for that image.'

'But you don't—or perhaps you do but you feel
I've overlooked you so you've put the defences up.'

She looked at him incredulously. Heavens, he was
some egocentric.

'I do my work well,' she told him tightly. 'You have no reason for complaint, I'm sure. I'm not naïve enough to think I have been invited down here for anything else but my work skills. You have an attitude with women and . . . and . . .'

'And you have no respect for me so therefore you feel free to voice your opinions quite openly.'

'I don't think I have voiced my opinions openly.'

'You called me a blood-starved vampire yesterday,' he reasoned humorously.

'Not without good reason,' she protested. 'Conrad would never have done what you did.'

'Because Conrad hasn't a caring bone in his body.'

Kate steeled herself at that insult to his brother. No, she couldn't imagine Conrad doing anything so blatantly intimate and maybe Guy had only done it to save her more hurt, but at the time she had seen it as a very sensual act. Oh, she didn't know what was happening to her. Guy Latham was an expert at throwing her completely.

'Maybe I'm so open with you because I know you have a track record with women and—'

'You don't know that; you are only repeating rumours.'

True. No one knew for sure his private life. She shrugged. 'I don't care, to be honest, but what I do care about is double standards. You operate them. You confuse me. We are sharing the same roof   and   you've . . . well . . . done . . . other things . . . and yet you expect me to show respect for you in a business sense. I do respect you as a boss but this isn't the Dark Ages where the employee is expected to touch his forelock whenever the boss shows his face.'

'Very true, but nevertheless you take enormous risks with me. I get the impression you are ambitious and yet you seem hell-bent on riling me at every opportunity. I hold the key to your future with this company and yet you take risks. I'm beginning to ask myself why.'

Kate screwed up her napkin and placed it on her plate, holding onto her temper by a hair's breadth. 'Perhaps I'm not as ambitious as you think. Perhaps I'm not willing to sleep with the boss to get what I want.'

She bit her lower lip and glanced at him hesitantly. That sounded awful, as if she had actually been considering it, and after last night he must think perhaps she had.

'I'm sorry. I shouldn't have said that,' she murmured.

'No, you shouldn't,' he agreed. 'But it's an interesting theory, another reason for showing an interest in my brother.'

Stunned, Kate opened her mouth to protest, but he gave her no chance. Slowly he pushed his chair back and stood up. He looked calm and what he had just said had come out *sounding* neutral, but she noticed a small nerve thrumming at his throat and gauged it to be a sign of repressed anger.

'I've already given you a warning in that direction, Kate,' he told her stiffly. 'Heed it or seek employment elsewhere because the way to promotion isn't via my brother's bedroom door.'

He left her stinging at the table, too shocked to respond. First she'd been a gold-digger and now she was a person willing to bed her way to promotion. She sat motionless, very aware that if he kept up his hurtful taunts she might let rip and end up jobless, with very little to show for all the hard work she had put in with the company since joining it.

But there was something worse thrumming away at her nerves. Guy Latham. He irritated her beyond sanity. She'd thought she knew him, had thought she had got his measure in the last nine months, but her assessment of him was all going awry. What he had done yesterday under the olive tree had shown that he had a few caring bones in *his* body, but what he had done last night had only confirmed that he was the opportunist she had always suspected. One sign of weakness on her part and he had been in there like a shot, taking advantage and then expecting her to be all moony about him this morning.

But she hadn't been moony, just confused, and in that confusion she was rubbing him up the wrong way. She had the ability to irritate him and that was a great surprise. Another great surprise was this lovely old house that he had put at her disposal. Charo had said no one was allowed here and he had thought she might appreciate its old-world charm, and the awful thing was that she did, but hadn't shown it.

'So what do I care?' she asked herself as she got up from the table and swept her bob back from her forehead, which was burning as if she had a fever. As she went upstairs to collect her bag she realised miserably that she did care that he thought she didn't appreciate this house and that she was an ambitious female willing to flirt with his brother to get a promotion. She loved this place, she *was* ambitious and if she had any interest in Conrad it was only because the man was so attractive and charming whereas his younger brother wasn't!

But it hadn't been the gorgeous Conrad who had smoothed the pain from her sunburnt thigh and made sure she got back to the house safely after drinking too much brandy last night, and it hadn't been Conrad who had kissed her so sensuously in the scented gardens on the way.

She shuddered inwardly as she hurried over to the villa and the office suite she had to spend hours in with Guy Latham. Perhaps the sun had gone to her head. Mediterranean madness, maybe. She loathed Guy Latham. She always had and she always would. No, nothing had changed.

CHAPTER FOUR

'THIS is the third mistake in as many days, Kate,' Guy grated at her impatiently, throwing the sheaf of contracts down on her console. 'And I said a dozen copies, not ten. Now correct those figures and let me have them at the speed of light. Understand?'

'Yes, I understand,' Kate murmured, and glowered at the screen of her computer. She understood very well that Guy was losing patience with her and she well understood what Lorraine was trying to do. Undermine her. These weren't her errors; they were Lorraine's. She had discreetly told her that because of the restructuring and redevelopment of these new contracts the output was increased, not decreased, hence the faulty figures. But Lorraine wouldn't listen and had said Conrad knew what he was talking about, and had added that ten copies were sufficient for Europe and not an old-fashioned British dozen.

And Kate was caught between all of them—because of Lorraine's relationship with Guy not able to speak up, because of Conrad's authority not even allowed to voice an opinion on his judgement to his younger brother. So she took it all, the glowering displeasure of everyone—except Conrad, who was being the perfect gentleman as usual. He had said if she had any problems to come to him, but how could she?

Just before lunch and siesta Kate spoke to Guy,
choosing a moment when he wasn't cradling a
phone to his ear and was rather idly gazing out of
the patio windows at the gardener tending the
potted geraniums. She'd noticed him doing that
occasionally over the last few days—sort of drifting
off into another world. But then the human dynamo
would crank up again and his work routine would
leave her breathless. The trouble was, he expected
her to keep up and the pressure was getting to her.

'Guy, is it possible for me to hire a car and...?
Well, I need to do some shopping and—'

He spun his chair round to look at her, his face
cold and expressionless. Crumbs, she wasn't asking
for much, surely? Just a little time to do some
shopping. Twice she'd had to wear the mink-
coloured silk. Last night Lorraine had tactlessly
asked her if that was the only dress she possessed,
although, thankfully, not in front of the Latham
brothers, which had rather surprised Kate. She'd.
had the ideal opportunity for an embarrassing put-
down there and Kate supposed she'd decided against
it because everything was going so well with her
and Guy.

Guy and Lorraine spent any spare time they had
with each other, leaving Kate to spend her siesta
time in the sanctuary of the old *finca*, and
Conrad... Kate didn't know what Conrad did in
his siesta time; he certainly hadn't suggested a swim
to her again after the initial offer.

'Charo is at your disposal for any personal
shopping you might need, Kate. Just give her a list
and she'll happily oblige. I need you here, not gal-
livanting around Puerto Banus. Now, is there any

chance you can have those corrections done before we break? They are urgent.' His tone was stiff and formal and Kate swallowed a protest.

He was being thoroughly unfair, over the last few days really exerting his boss mode, issuing her with a mobile phone so she could take calls during siesta—not that there were any, because the whole of Spain knocked off for a few hours in the heat of the afternoon.

Charo couldn't buy her a couple of new dresses. What did it matter anyway? A hell of a lot actually. Going shopping would mean more than just the purchase of a new outfit to make her not feel at such a disadvantage. She was stifling in this rigid routine. She had honestly expected a little time of her own to get out and see a bit of Andalusia apart from Caesar's palace next door. But, as Guy had said, this wasn't Club Med but a place of work. Pity he didn't think of that when he and Lorraine swanned off together in the Mercedes every afternoon.

'Charo, do you think you could get me some toiletries? I'm out of shampoo already,' she asked her when she got back to the guest house. She hadn't expected to have to wash her hair twice a day. The heat was playing havoc with her normally sleek bob.

'Of course, but the local shops are closed for siesta. You could come with me down to Marbella Town. The shops stay open for tourists there.'

'I'd love to,' Kate told her, 'but I have to be here. The phone.' She slumped down at the table under the shady vines and Charo poured her a glass of freshly squeezed orange juice.

'Señor Latham work you too hard,' she commented drily. 'The other, she out every day.'

Kate smiled ruefully. 'That's life.' She sensed that Charo had warmed to her more than to the crisp Lorraine, but of course she couldn't say anything against Lorraine.

'Why you no swim in the pool? Every afternoon you stay here. It too hot. You should swim.'

Kate sipped her juice. 'Yes, I will this afternoon,' she said, making the decision to do just that. Conrad had offered her the use of the pool, after all. But would Guy object? She thought about it briefly and then wondered why she should consider what he thought anyway. She could take the mobile with her. 'Yes, I will,' she repeated, getting up and already looking forward to it.

It was delicious. Kate swam three lengths of the pool and then hung on the side, shaking her auburn hair back from her face and floating, kicking her long legs in the cool water. Amazingly she was getting a tan already, even though she had scarcely exposed herself to the sun after that unfortunate accident of falling asleep in the garden.

'You swim very well,' she heard from above her. 'I'm glad you've lost your inhibitions at last and joined me.'

Kate trod water and twisted round to look back. Conrad towered above her, his body lean and taut in white swimming shorts. He was smiling down at her and then he stretched and arched his body and dived into the pool, swimming strongly and powerfully to the other end. Kate watched him in silence as he turned and swam gracefully back to her. Inhibitions, she mused. She supposed he was right.

She had been rather slow in coming forward with everyone but Guy. But things hadn't been too bad these last few days, putting aside Guy's hostility and Lorraine's little put-downs.

She wondered why Conrad had never married. He had so much to offer. She reckoned him to be approaching his forties but sometimes men of his success and status left it late in life to marry and start a family. She admired a man like that, one who knew exactly where he was going in life.

'A drink?' he suggested, hauling himself out of the pool and reaching down to offer her his hand.

Kate took it and he swung her up out of the water, as effortlessly as if she were a water nymph. She felt heat course through her as he hung onto her hand a little longer than was necessary. Shyly she turned away to reach for her towel on a lounger.

As she towel-dried her hair she heard him calling for drinks.

'So, little Kate, tell me all about yourself. When I took you out to dinner last month we didn't get off the subject of business. We scarcely got to know each other.' He settled in a lounger and nodded to her to sit down at the one beside him, under the welcome shade of a huge parasol.

Steeling herself against 'little Kate', she sank down and stretched her long legs out and patted them dry with the towel. The drinks arrived on a silver tray, two long glasses of lemonade with twists of lemon and tinkling ice, delivered by a young man who looked remarkably like Charo and gave her a beaming smile. She took one of the glasses—and nearly choked, gin biting at the back of her throat. The gin was too much for her on a hot afternoon beside the man she so admired. She set it down on the low table beside her, hoping he wouldn't notice she wasn't drinking it.

The time passed far too quickly, Conrad showing the caring ability to draw her out. He asked about her life and what she did in her spare time and she told him about her flat in Bracknell and the health club she belonged to and how her mother always came to stay when she was in England. And then she found herself telling him about the break-up of her parents' marriage.

'And no brothers and sisters to commiserate with,' he sympathised.

'No,' she said sadly, wishing there had been because at times she felt very insular. She had a few friends, but all of them were from the club and none of them were intimate friends she could confide in.

'A bad thing, a marriage breaking up,' he said mournfully. 'Makes you wary of a relationship yourself.'

Oh, yes, how right he was. She'd known he would be the sort to understand.

'So, an education in Switzerland and a youth spent travelling with your mother in Europe. A travel writer, you say. You must have had quite a life with her. So you aren't the innocent you look.'

Kate knew she would have been riled if Guy had spoken those same words because Guy would have added a tone of innuendo to them. She frowned suddenly. She shouldn't compare the two and wondered why she had. Conrad was a real man, mature and so very easy to talk to because he knew how to treat a woman.

'I hear good reports of you from my brother,' Conrad went on. Kate dug her fingers into her palms. It was funny how he could give good reports to his brother but rake her over the coals when she was *supposed* be have made a mistake. 'He thinks very highly of you,' Conrad went on, lifting a fresh glass of gin and tonic to his lips. 'I expect that makes you feel good, doesn't it?'

The question took her aback for a brief second. It sounded as if he was fishing to find out how she felt about his brother. And then her heart started to race. Yes, perhaps he was, because he was such a gentleman that he wouldn't like to tread on his brother's toes if she had any feelings for Guy.

'Guy and I have a good working relationship,' she told him warily, and then flushed as he watched her intently, waiting for more. She couldn't offer more, though. How could she tell him that his brother drove her to despair, irritated her more than was good for her and was everything she didn't like in a man?

She shifted uncomfortably on the lounger. 'I'd better get back,' she murmured, and swung her legs over the side of the lounger to get up.

Conrad suddenly reached out and tapped her thigh lightly. 'I've enjoyed our chat, Kate. You'll go a long way in this company if you keep your wits about you.'

Kate stood up and smiled down at him. 'I won't deny I'm ambitious, Conrad. I very much enjoy my work and I want to get on and I'm very grateful for this opportunity to be here.'

He laughed. 'Yes, quite. I'm very glad my brother picked you for the job. You're an asset—a very beautiful asset, I must add.'

He held her dark eyes with his, just long enough for a thrill of pleasure to run down Kate's spine—to replace the icy reminder that had gone before. Yes, it was Guy who had chosen her, and because her work was so good and nothing personal, as he had so scathingly told her.

'Kate.' Conrad spoke softly, just as the white Mercedes came purring up the pink gravel driveway, thrumming to a halt in full view of the pool.

Kate felt her back stiffen. Why did Guy Latham have that effect on her, making her tense warily at the sight of him? He got out of the car and looked over to the pool and she could see the cold displeasure in his eyes. She felt like a prisoner caught out of her cell without permission.

'Kate, we must do this again; I've so enjoyed it.'

Conrad's voice was but a murmur in the middle distance as Lorraine's burst of laughter winged its way into the air. Kate narrowed her eyes against the sun, watching as Lorraine hauled packages out from the car with her. Designer-labelled packages.

'I . . . I beg your pardon?' Kate uttered, screwing up the corner of her towel and turning back to Conrad to give him her attention.

Conrad was suddenly standing next to her, taking the towel from her stiffened fingers and draping it around her shoulders. To her astonishment he turned her head to look into her eyes, tilting her chin to do it. She felt the smooth touch of his fingers on her chin and at the same time almost physically felt the pierce of Guy's eyes in the small of her back. It sent a sharp, icy sliver of awareness down her spine.

'I said we must do this again,' he said quietly. 'I've enjoyed it, and don't forget if there is anything I can do to make your stay with us more pleasant you only have to ask.'

As Kate met his dark, smoky eyes she heard the resounding slam of a car door echoing across the pool. It made her blink and jarred at her spine again and she resented the fact that Guy could disturb her so. She smiled at Conrad as she came to a swift decision.

'As a matter of fact, Conrad, I've been meaning to ask you... I hope you won't think it an imposition, but I'd like to hire a car one afternoon. I need to do some shopping and—'

'And it would be my pleasure to escort you,' Conrad murmured. He smiled. 'I'm glad you asked.'

Kate opened her mouth to protest that a hire car would be sufficient and then she bit the inner flesh of her lip. Why not? Why not let Conrad accompany her? Guy and Lorraine were out every afternoon and why shouldn't she have some freedom?

'Thank you,' she murmured. 'I look forward to that.'

She turned away, picked up the mobile phone from the low table, and, clutching it tightly, walked stiffly away towards the side of the villa, back to what she had once thought her sanctuary. So why wasn't she walking on cloud nine? Conrad was taking her out, away from here, probably down to

Puerto Banús and the glittering shops, and she would have him all to herself and . . .

'And I'm not walking on air,' she muttered to herself. 'I'm scared—not of Conrad; he's a darling. So what are you scared of, idiot Stephens?' The wrath of Guy Latham, that was what.

'Any phone calls?' Guy asked, perfectly matter-of-factly.

He'd stepped into the cool dimness of the house only seconds after her. Kate was at the fridge, taking out a bottle of water to take away the bitterness of the gin which still lingered in her mouth.

She slammed the fridge door shut, wondering why she felt a prickle of anger at such a simple question. The truth was, she had expected him to make some sort of derisive remark about seeing her by the pool with the brother he had warned her off. So why the prickle of anger when he hadn't? She poured herself a glass of water. Probably because she had prepared herself for a row and he wasn't giving her cause for one.

'There never are any at this time of day,' she told him shortly.

'But there might be,' he said, and reached for the water bottle.

'Whoever invented the telephone answering machine needn't have bothered,' she told him drily.

She handed him a glass from the cupboard above her head. The towel around her shoulders slipped and she hauled it back, too late to prevent him getting a good look at her bikini-clad figure. She saw his eyes darken for a fraction of a second and it made her feel shivery and vulnerable. Kate tightened the towel around her, clutched the ends at her chin with one hand and sipped her water with the other.

'Faced with an answering machine, would you leave a million-pound order on it?' He didn't give her time to reply but went on, 'It's what you're here for, Kate. The personal touch on the end of the line.'

'Sales are nothing to do with me. I'm not marketing manager but I know someone who is!' she retorted, and told herself that if he didn't know who she meant then he ought to. She finished her water and put the glass down.

He eyed her darkly. 'You want promotion, don't you?'

'Yes, but—'

'But nothing. You come up through the ranks and that means doing as you are told.'

'Yes, sir!' she bit out, and even had the effrontery to touch her forelock with her free hand. She really did amaze herself at times. She was on a roller coaster of self-destruction every time he was around and she couldn't stop it.

His fingers tightened around the glass he was holding. 'And what brought that on?' he asked.

'Unfair treatment,' she told him honestly, lifting her chin to show she meant business. 'It seems the marketing manager gets perks that aren't offered to the rest of the staff.'

'The other staff being your own sweet self, I suppose?'

Kate glanced around the room as if looking for other bodies. 'I don't see anyone else around,' she said sarcastically.

Kate revelled in the fact that she could annoy him. There was that pulse thrumming away at his throat to accompany his white knuckles.

'You really do push your luck at times, Kate.'

'I'm not pushing my luck. Only expecting to be treated fairly. I'm sure if I delved deep enough I might find something in the European statutory terms of agreement of employment that allows me some free time to myself.'

'You have every afternoon free to rest—'

'Yes, rest. After all the work I put in I certainly need it, but that isn't the point. I asked for permission to hire a car to do some shopping and—'

'And Charo is at your disposal—'

'And you are at Lorraine's,' she bit back, and instantly wished that she had kept this feeling of discontent inside her. The trouble was, this was all at the root of it. He and Lorraine whooshed off every afternoon and that just wasn't fair.

'So jealousy rears its ugly head, does it?'

'It does not!' she exploded, furious at his derisive, presumptuous tone and that damned glittering look of amusement in his eyes.

She swung round to the sink, furiously rinsed her glass out under the tap and stared idiotically through the window overlooking the shady courtyard. Heat rose up from her bare feet and fired her nerve-endings. Jealousy? Oh, no. It wasn't possible; it just wasn't! So what exactly had she felt by the pool when the two beautiful people had returned from a shopping trip to Puerto Banus?

I'm going mad. Kate squirmed inwardly. Right off of my trolley in this heat. She licked her lips and turned to face him, fighting for her senses to return to normal. She *was not* jealous of Lorraine.

'What is good for Lorraine should be good enough for me,' she reasoned in a small voice. Oh, no, wrong choice of words, she thought. That glittering humour in his eyes was turning into a very knowing look.

'Well, I'm sure that can be arranged if you drop that defensiveness of yours,' he grated suggestively.

She went hot at the thought. 'You know exactly what I'm talking about, Guy. I don't want the sort of personal favours you lavish on Lorraine, thank you, but I want fair treatment.'

He drained his glass and set it down in the sink, having to lean close to her to do it. Kate tensed and tightened her grip on the towel under her chin. His eyes were on a level with hers, cold and unyielding now.

'Well, you've made a good start, sweetheart. Already my brother is eating out of your hand— or did I misinterpret that intimacy I witnessed at the poolside just now? Perhaps you are eating out of *his* to get what you want.'

Kate drew in a sharp breath and then let it out with a vengeance. 'I wonder if you would dare say that if your brother was standing here?'

'I wonder if you would be clutching at that towel quite so primly if he was?' he grated back at her.

The shock of that cruel jibe stung Kate so painfully that it took her breath away. Why had he the power to hurt her so? She didn't even like him. Suddenly his hand came up and wrenched at the towel so unexpectedly that she didn't have a chance to clutch at it.

His eyes raked her up and down once he had revealed her near-nakedness. Kate stiffened her back against the sink and held her breath, so many emotions quickening her pulse rate that she thought he couldn't fail to notice the effect he had on her. And I don't even like him, her inner voice repeated as his eyes settled on the rise of her cleavage from her red bikini-top. So why did she feel as if a fire had been ignited inside her? Why did she feel as if her skin had been grazed by a brand? Why, oh, why was her heart thudding so?

'And very nice, too,' he said smoothly, raising his eyes to meet hers and holding them, defying her to look away. 'For once in his life my brother is showing some taste, but don't let it go to your head, sweetheart. I warned you about the games he plays, didn't I?'

Slowly and determinedly Kate reached for the towel he was holding in his left hand. Once she had hold of it she jerked it sharply, but he was just a shade quicker than her and gave it a counter-tug which jerked her towards him. Her chin caught his shoulder and she let out a gasp—a gasp he turned to his advantage by covering her parted lips with his own.

Humiliation was the first emotion that slapped at her, and then a strange, strange feeling took its place. A swimming euphoria swamped her, sending her drifting off into the unknown. Guy was doing it again—undermining her grasp on reality, kissing her passionately, now tossing aside the towel to grasp her firmly and without encumbrance against his hard body.

His heat and power were everything—something she wanted to repel but couldn't. She felt the warm silk of his shirt against her breasts and the roughness of his linen trousers against the thigh he had soothed so expertly days ago—days in which the memory of the sensation of his fingers on her flesh had plagued her.

No, this was impossible; this wasn't happening. She tore her fevered mouth from his and gasped for air, and then he was holding her firmly by the shoulders and looking at her, deep into her eyes. He parted his lips to speak and the words that came out seemed to hang ominously in the hot air.

'If I ever have reason to believe you kiss my brother like this I'll have you on the first plane back to Heathrow with your dismissal tucked in that scented cleavage of yours.'

He let her go, brutally, in contrast to the sensuality of his kisses. It was just what she needed to spur her anger to her lips.

'Why wait, Guy Latham?' she said brazenly, her dark eyes narrowing. 'You were out a long time this afternoon, long enough—'

His eyes darkened to jet, so terrifyingly quickly that Kate regretted her stab at him. She moved then, jerked herself away from between him and the sink, just at the moment that the arched door out in the courtyard banged open.

'Señor Latham!' Charo called.

Guy caught Kate's arm as she was about to tear out of the kitchen and up to her room. He swung her back to face him.

'Don't you ever throw something like that at me again. You belittle yourself—'

'Well, I won't do it again,' she interjected fiercely through her teeth. 'Why do something myself when *you* are around to do it better? You obviously have a very poor opinion of me, which proves you aren't too choosy. Remember that when you consider kissing me again!'

She flew then, passing Charo in the sitting room.

'Your shampoo,' Charo called, but the last thing on Kate's mind was the state of her hair. Dear God, but she wouldn't have any left by the time this assignment was over!

She ran into the bathroom and locked the door. Damn you, Guy Latham, she silently raged. Shakily she ran a warm shower and stood under it for ages, hating the feel of that kiss still burning her lips, hating and hating this raging inside her. She hated him and yet . . . he'd just melted her bones, sent her pulses racing, her heart thudding. Attraction? Sexual chemistry? *No way*—and she wasn't jealous of those trips he took with Lorraine every afternoon, just envious that Lorraine was allowed out while she was chained to the mobile phone.

Conrad wouldn't treat her so abominably—never. He was a gentleman, a real man, a caring man, and damn, damn his brother.

'I'm eating here tonight. Charo is cooking for me and—'

'And for me,' Guy told her as he stepped into the sitting room.

Kate was coiled on a sofa, flicking through a magazine and waiting for him to appear so that she could tell him. They had worked through the after-siesta session with the minimum of exchanges of words, the atmosphere between them so strained that Kate had decided she would rather eat at the guest house than suffer a night of his black looks on the terrace of the villa. She had asked Charo if that would be all right and Charo had said something like it was arranged anyway, but Kate had thought she'd misheard because Charo couldn't have known her intention beforehand.

Kate flattened the magazine on her lap and looked at him. He wasn't dressed for dinner and neither was she. She'd flung on a cotton sundress as she'd thought she would be dining alone. He had changed into light-coloured chinos and a short-sleeved navy silk shirt.

'There is no need to join me, Guy. I'm not planning a clandestine meeting with your brother here,' she told him thinly, and picked up the magazine again.

'I know you're not. He's dining out tonight,' he told her as he went through to the courtyard to speak to Charo who was preparing the table outside. He came back, via the kitchen, with two glasses of chilled white wine, gave her one and then sat across from her in a leather chair by the white-washed fireplace.

'Don't you want to know more?'

Kate put the magazine down beside her and sipped her wine before speaking. 'Is there more?' She wondered what he was getting at.

'Plenty more if you're interested, which I'm sure you are in spite of that look of boredom on your face.'

'If I'm looking bored it's in anticipation of you joining me for dinner. I'd planned an evening of my own company, which would have proved far more entertaining.'

He smiled above his wineglass. 'You really do walk the tightrope at times, Kate.'

'You set the tone of our relationship, Guy. If you go around kissing your employees you can't expect respect.'

'So, did you lose respect for my brother—?'

'Your brother hasn't laid a finger on me,' she interrupted him before he could go any further along that particular tightrope.

'Yet,' Guy added meaningfully.

Kate lowered her eyes to her wineglass. Here we go again, she mused. 'I'm not a gold-digger,' she told him quietly but firmly. 'I'm not interested in your brother for his wealth.'

'What exactly do you see in him, then—some sort of father-figure?'

Kate shot him a look of disbelief. 'Father-figure?'

Guy shrugged. 'If it's not the money it's reasonable to assume your interest in an older man is—'

Trying to suppress the blush that was coming to her face, she blurted out, 'That's ridiculous! Anyway, he's not a lot older and—' That sounded like confirmation that she was interested in Conrad, she realised.

'Twenty years older than you, Kate,' he told her knowingly. 'Old enough to be your father. Have you got one, by the way?'

'Got what?'

'A father.'

'Of course I've got a father. Everyone's got a father. Except you, possibly,' she added for insult.

She swallowed a gulp of wine. That was an insult he would surely sack her on the spot for. Pity she hadn't called him a bastard and been done with it. But he didn't rise to it, though Kate knew for sure that he hadn't missed the point. He seemed amused by it more than anything.

'Is this father of yours apparent?'

'Is this any of your business?' she asked scathingly.

'You don't want to talk about him, then?'

Kate swung her legs off the sofa and was about to get up when he held up his hand.

'OK, OK. I've touched a sore point. I apologise.'

Kate sat back and glared at him. 'It is not a sore point,' she told him tightly. 'And I haven't any hang-ups about him. I never see my father because he left my mother for another woman when I was four. I wouldn't know him if he walked into this room now. I can't remember him. I'm not interested in him. He doesn't exist for me. Now, does that satisfy your curiosity?'

'It answers what I've come to suspect, Kate.'

'Oh, yes, and what is that?'

'If you're not after his money then you see my brother as a father-figure. Don't be ashamed of it,' he assured her quickly. 'It's a fairly classic syndrome.'

Kate was on her feet now, glaring at him across the dimly lit sitting room, hating him for that very suggestion.

'I am not a "classic syndrome"!' she stormed. 'If—and just if—I have any feelings for your brother they are born of respect and admiration for him—something that I don't have very much of for you!'

'I won't lose any sleep over that.'

'I wouldn't expect you to, and while we are on the subject of sleep I'd rather do that than share the dinner table with you tonight and because I am off duty now I don't feel obliged to ask to be excused!'

'You do as you are told, Kate,' he announced stiffly, getting to his feet and coming towards her.

Kate froze, praying he wasn't going to do something crazy like kissing her into submission. She wouldn't be able to stand another close encounter.

He stood before her, not attempting to touch her but nevertheless holding her rigid to the spot with his eye contact.

'You are not excused,' he said determinedly. 'You are dining with me tonight if I have to strap you to your chair and force-feed you.'

Kate lifted her chin. He had to be joking. 'I will not!'

He grasped her defiant chin before she could escape. His voice was low as he grated, 'You will, sweetheart, but don't take it personally. Frankly I'd rather dine with swine than have to face your insults across the table but the choice isn't mine any more.' His voice suddenly went lower till it was almost a whisper. 'Charo has prepared us a typical Andalusian meal tonight and neither you nor I are going to insult her by sloping off to bed before we have eaten every last scrap. Got the message?'

Oh, she had the message all right. He wanted her company as much as she wanted his. But what had she expected? You couldn't go around jibing at the man you most hated in the world and expect him to put up with it for very long before returning that hatred.

'I . . . I understand,' she uttered weakly. But she didn't. She didn't understand why she should suddenly feel so very let down.

But as his hand dropped to his side and he turned away to gather up their wineglasses she suddenly did understand.

Guy Latham exasperated her, drove her wild with fury most of the time, and yet . . . he had the power to . . . to excite her. And when it came that excitement superseded all those negative impulses he drew from her. Yes, he excited her, and wasn't that very interesting . . . ?

CHAPTER FIVE

BECAUSE of, and only because of Charo's feelings, Kate followed him out to the pretty courtyard where candles flickered and threw fascinating shadows on the rough white walls.

She sat down under the trailing vines and gazed at the lovely table covered in white lace and set with sparkling crystal and bright silver cutlery. Hibiscus flower-heads swam in a shallow bowl of water at the centre and it all looked beautifully seductive. The scents of Spain assailed her, jasmine and ripening grapes, peppery and sweet. The buzz of cicadas filled the hot night air.

It was a secret place for lovers and Kate wished... For a moment that wish hung over her uncertainly. Did she really wish she had a lover, even wish to put *Guy* in the seat of this imaginary lover? He was sitting across from her, watching her threateningly, daring her to make it awkward for Charo by sulking through the meal. She knew in that raw moment that she wanted peace of mind above all things, but was that possible with this uncertainty pressing at her?

'Why so solemn?' Guy asked at last as he poured the wine.

Kate stared at the asparagus dish that Charo had just set so proudly before them before discreetly disappearing into the kitchen again. It looked delicious and she so wanted to enjoy it, for Charo's sake. She toyed with her fork as she raised limpid brown eyes to his.

'Was this all your idea?' she asked in a soft voice.

'Yes,' he told her sincerely, his voice very low. 'An extension of what I have offered you already.'

Her heart pounded. She realised he had offered her so much. A chance to come down here and work with him, this lovely house to stay in, both of which she had believed were Conrad's ideas. She had been so very wrong in both assumptions, so how could she trust her judgement in anything else? She had come here admiring his brother and hating him but now her feelings were getting very scary.

'Why?'

'You already know. I thought you would appreciate it. So many people come to Spain and never see the charm and reality of it.'

'This is hardly the real Spain,' she argued, but not in anger. 'Just around the corner is . . . is—'

'Caesar's palace?' he prompted.

She smiled and nodded.

'But I preserved this old *finca*. When we bought it years ago Conrad was all for rolling it over but I wanted it kept more or less as it was. It had no electricity, no plumbing and was very basic, and I had to bow to some sort of modernisation—sympathetically, I hope.'

'It's beautiful,' Kate murmured, and started to eat.

'So you do appreciate it after all.'

'I never said I didn't. I was overwhelmed that first day,' she admitted. 'I thought—' She stopped. How could she tell him she had been thrilled because she'd thought Conrad had arranged it for her?

'You thought what?'

Kate shrugged. 'It doesn't matter.' She paused and looked up at him again. 'That first day Charo said I was lucky because no one came here; you didn't allow people here.'

'I've never had any member of the London staff here because I've never thought any of them capable of appreciating it. Say "Marbella" to any of them and they immediately think jet-set villas and glittering nightclubs.'

'You didn't know I wouldn't think likewise,' she told him, reaching for her wine but not immediately lifting it to her lips.

'I did.'

'Go on,' she prompted, though her heart was thudding again at what he might say.

'Your nine months with the company haven't gone completely unnoticed by me, you know.'

His dark eyes locked with hers but Kate couldn't hold the gaze. She looked away, concentrated on a tiny gecko heading up the wall to the candle-sconce. Guy had noticed her and she hadn't thought he had and days ago she wouldn't have cared. Now it was so different. She felt extremely hot and fazed and gulped at her wine.

'You're not a mixer, Kate. That has always intrigued me.'

The wine steadied her. She knew it wouldn't go to her head. So she intrigued him. It was easy to understand all this now. She *was* a challenge to him. For some unaccountable reason she felt a thread of disappointment draw through her.

'Yes, I suppose it must have done,' she told him tightly.

'So why?' he asked.

'Why what?'

'Why don't you mix?'

She put her fork down, feeling uncomfortable. She had never thought of herself as a non-mixer. 'I do. I arrive at work and I talk about the weather and everything else people gossip about first thing in the morning and then I get down to my work because that is what I'm paid to do.'

'Lorraine tells me—'

She didn't let him finish. The mention of Lorraine stung her. 'Lorraine gossips about things that don't appeal to me,' she cut in shortly.

He ignored her remark and leaned across the table to top up her wine. 'Lorraine tells me,' he went on as if she hadn't spoken, 'that you are very good at your work but sadly lacking in social skills.'

'No,' Kate retorted. 'Correction. Gossip, not social skills. I know exactly how to behave in any *social* situation. What grieves Lorraine is that I don't gossip behind people's backs like everyone else does.'

'Gossip is the lifeblood of every social gathering, whether it be at work or at leisure. It's a safety-valve, you know. You'd go crackers without it.'

Kate stared at him in disbelief, not sure if he was serious or not. His eyes were suddenly glinting with humour so she decided this was his way of lightening the conversation.

She half smiled. 'Interesting theory.'

'Very interesting, and true. It's built into us. Newspapers thrive on it and wouldn't sell a single copy if the public didn't lap it up so. I'd say you have a problem if you don't take it for what it is.'

'A safety-valve, you mean?'

He nodded and leaned back as Charo came through from the kitchen to take away their dishes. Kate looked down at her plate and found it was empty, although she hadn't realised she had eaten it all.

'That was delicious, Charo. Thank you,' she murmured to her in Spanish.

Charo beamed and went inside for the next course.

'Yes, you do have social graces,' Guy told her with a smile.

'But I don't gossip, which according to you has me halfway to the funny farm.'

He laughed and her pulses sped because when he laughed he was even more attractive. 'I didn't say that—or did I?'

'I think you implied it.' She smiled. 'Would I get my promotion if I kowtowed to gossip and joined in, did what everyone else does and gossiped about who's bedding who within the company?'

'I'm sure if you were involved you'd be very capable of holding your own.'

Kate felt that was a compliment and it glowed inside her.

'But you wouldn't feel comfortable doing it, would you?' he added.

'I'm not a part of it.'

'So you feel left out?'

Kate's eyes narrowed. 'No, I don't feel left out,' she protested. 'You know, you amaze me. You of all people should be above all this and yet you are no different; you actually enjoy all this gossip, don't you? And Lorraine Hunter is your little quisling, aiding the enemy.'

'On the contrary, I am above it all, but I have to listen when things are put to me. I wouldn't be a fair employer if I didn't take it all in my stride, albeit gossip.' He leaned forward and captured her eyes with his. '"Aiding the enemy". Am I the enemy?'

There was a loaded question, if she took it personally and answered it from the heart. She avoided the personal touch.

'No, of course not, but you know what I mean. You're the boss.'

'And usually the meat of most of the gossip,' he said with humour.

'Well, you ask for that.' Kate laughed. 'All macho magnetism and broody undertones.'

'I can't change the way I am and wouldn't if I could. I keep my staff buzzing and on their pretty little toes and striving to please. It's good for production. I'd say that was commendable marketing, wouldn't you?'

'From your point of view maybe, but I see it as sexism with fascist undertones. Do you wield that dangerous but desirable attitude with the male employees with equal determination? No, I think not.'

Guy was still laughing when Charo brought out the next course.

'Pork with Málaga wine,' she announced with a smile. 'You will love the wine sauce, señorita. It is the taste of Málaga sunshine.'

'With the kick of an Andalusian mule,' Guy added, and Charo laughed and went back inside for the vegetables.

'You can go now, Charo,' he told her when she had placed dishes of green beans and braised artichokes at the centre of the table for them to help themselves.

Kate had never given a thought to the fact that Charo wasn't on the premises all the time. Now it hit her with the kick of that Andalusian mule Guy had mentioned. Every night she and Guy were alone here. He in his bedroom, she in hers. So why worry about it now? She watched him as he served up the vegetables for her and her thoughts went to Lorraine who adored him so. If she were here, surely they would be sharing the same bedroom?

Kate's stomach seemed to fold in on her at the thought of Guy and Lorraine sharing a bed. How would she feel if she were over at the villa with Conrad and Lorraine were here every night with Guy? It was a question she'd have thought she would never have cause to ask herself. Very, very unsteadily Kate reached for her wine. This wasn't possible, this tightening inside her.

'Lorraine,' she forced out from between white lips. 'Where is she this evening?' She could just imagine how she must be feeling, knowing Guy was sharing an intimate supper with her while she was at the villa on her own: very put down.

'Lorraine is out,' Guy said softly, and then he raised his eyes from the vegetable dishes to lock with hers. 'Out with my brother,' he added.

Kate swallowed. She hadn't expected that, not at all. And she wished she hadn't asked because now she knew what all this was about and it thrust an unwelcome disappointment at her. Guy hadn't planned this intimate supper for her benefit as he had said. He didn't even want to be here, but he was because he had no one else to dine with tonight.

'Why no comment?' he asked.

'What can I say?' she murmured, eyes lowered. 'It's nothing to do with me.'

He said nothing and they ate in silence. She felt his eyes on her, though, searching for signs of jealousy, she supposed, because tonight had given him another opportunity to put her off his brother, this time using Lorraine as the cause. So Lorraine and Conrad were dining out together. Remarkably Kate didn't care a jot. She was curious, though. Guy was showing no sign of jealousy, which prompted her next brave question.

'So how do you feel about it?'

'Lorraine out with my brother? He can look after himself,' he said nonchalantly, and carried on eating.

'Interesting,' Kate mused, and he looked up quizzically. Kate went on, 'Interesting choice of gender. *He* can look after himself. After all your warnings to me about your brother and the games he plays and always wins, surely you should show some concern for Lorraine? Sounds to me as if you think she is the predator and not him.'

He sighed. 'Perhaps I should have worded it better. Try this for size. *They* can look after themselves.'

Kate frowned. 'You don't care, do you? You don't care that Lorraine is out with your brother.'

He shrugged slightly. 'Should I?'

Kate let go of her fork and it clattered against her plate. She took a deep breath because this was a situation she didn't understand. 'You and

Lorraine...' Her voice trailed off. He and Lorraine were an item, surely?

'Go on,' he urged, giving her his full attention across the table. 'You do have an annoying habit of leaving sentences incomplete.'

'Because you confuse me,' she protested. 'I thought you and Lorraine were...well...you know...sort of together, and now she is out with your brother and—'

'And you are here with me,' he interjected.

'And we wouldn't be together if they weren't,' she told him.

'And they wouldn't be together if we weren't.'

'Guy, you are being difficult,' Kate gasped in exasperation.

'No, Kate, you are. I think you should take up gossip as a hobby because it might help you to be more forthcoming. You are going all round the houses trying to find out what you really want to know, which is whether or not there is something going on between my brother and Lorraine which might interfere with your intentions towards Conrad. I'm right, aren't I?'

Kate stared at him hard across the table. This was ridiculous! Yes, very ridiculous because he was very wrong. She admired Conrad greatly and perhaps she had indulged in the odd fantasy now and again, but really it meant nothing. But why tell him that? Why lay open her feelings and emotions for him to pick holes in? He'd already had a good stab at them.

'No comment,' she told him defiantly, and his eyes flashed with anger for a second and then he shrugged as if it wasn't important anyway.

No comment! Why had she been so final when really what she still wanted to know more than anything in the world was the answer to the chicken-and-egg syndrome? Which had come first, Guy's intention to dine with her leaving Conrad and Lorraine free to do their own thing, or Lorraine and Conrad's intention to dine out, leaving Guy to do his own thing?

I want to know, she thought heatedly. I want to know if this is more than he's making out, more than wanting to show me the real Spain.

He had kissed her and she was sharing this lovely house with him and she intrigued him because she didn't mix and... and did he see her as a challenge? She didn't fall rapt at his feet like all the others. She always kept herself to herself, so was there some truth in Lorraine's accusation that she was holding back from him in the hope of gaining his attention? Was she unwittingly playing the oldest game in the world, issuing Guy Latham with some sort of silent challenge?

'Do you have a man in your life, Kate?' he unexpectedly asked.

Kate nearly choked. His unpredictability never ceased to shock her.

'No, I don't, and before you ask the question on the tip of your tongue I'll tell you why. I avoid men like I would avoid the plague if there was an outbreak because I don't trust them.'

'I thought that must be the explanation for your wariness with me. What happened? Did he jilt you?'

He wasn't teasing her or mocking her so she told him the truth. 'It didn't get that far. I wasn't enough for him. He was running around with other women and I was the last to know. Classic syndrome—bruised ego, once bitten, twice shy, et cetera, and to add insult to injury my mother postscripted the whole affair with an ''I told you so''.' Kate shrugged. 'She knew from past experience, of course.'

Guy was silent for a while and then he murmured, 'One mistake shouldn't put you off trying again.'

'But it does,' she admitted pensively. She brightened herself up with a smile. 'So now you know my life history.'

'More wine?' Guy breathed.

Kate gazed at her wineglass. It had been topped up so many times, she didn't know how much she had drunk.

'No, thank you,' she murmured. 'I've had quite enough.'

Enough for her to have revealed her innermost feelings about men to him and enough for it to have sharpened her awareness that Guy Latham was a very attractive man, an interesting man, a fascinating man. Had she known all along? Sadly the wine hadn't honed that question to knife-edged sharpness. But now, at this moment in time, was she dangerously attracted to him?

'I'll make coffee,' she said quickly, and stood up, her thigh jarring on the old wooden table—the thigh he had so sensitively balmed that day she had fallen asleep in the sun. There had been no after-effects on her skin but she couldn't deny the after-effects on her emotions. His touch had seared her senses more than anything, exposed a deep need she hadn't thought she possessed.

'I'll help,' he said, and went to get up, but Kate stopped him, reaching out her hand to touch his shoulder, retracting it swiftly as she realised it was the first voluntary movement she had made towards him. He caught her eye as if he knew what had flashed through her mind and then he smiled and she knew he had.

She gathered up the dirty dishes and went into the house, leaving him in the sweetly scented courtyard. Her hands shook as she filled a pan of water for the coffee. She was way out of her depth and fortunately recognised it. Games and challenges were out of her league. She didn't know how to play even if she wanted to.

So abstinence was the only answer, coupled with a sharp reminder to herself that Guy Latham was still the same man she had despised for so long in spite of this crazy feeling inside her now. He was still a guy with a mega-sized ego, a reputation for being a heartbreaker, not the sort of man to be trusted further than you could throw him. He was typical of most men—men like wretched Gustav and her father, who had broken her mother's heart. They were all the same.

'Whatever is that?' she asked in astonishment as she came out into the courtyard with the tray of coffee and a plate of small sweet pastries that Charo had left out for them.

'Old Chinese game—Jenga. A test of dexterity and steadiness of hand,' Guy told her, stacking layers of three wooden blocks at right angles to each other to form a tower on the table. 'Each player has to extract a block from the tower and then place it on the top without toppling it, using only one hand. If you topple it you lose. Loser restacks the blocks as a penalty.'

Smiling, Kate poured coffee and handed him his. 'Sounds too easy to me and hardly the kind of challenge I would have thought you would rise to.'

He held her eyes with his and it was as if he knew she had been thinking of games and challenges while she had been making the coffee. She looked away and stemmed the hot tide of heat that rose to her throat. She sat down across from him and studied the blocks. This sort of tabletop game she could cope with.

'Challenges come in different forms, Kate,' he said softly, concentrating on the tower between them. 'But then you know that, don't you?'

Kate didn't miss the innuendo in his rhetorical question and she felt a stab of hurt. So it was true; she was a game to him, nothing more, nothing less.

'Your move,' he prompted after expertly removing the first block and placing it at the top of the stack.

'You have the advantage of having played before,' she murmured as she studied the blocks, deciding which one would be the safest to remove. 'But,' she added, meaningfully trading innuendoes, 'I'm a quick learner and have a determination not to be beaten. But then you know that, don't you?'

His soft laughter rose up into the hot, balmy Mediterranean night, and later, when Kate lay sleepless in her bed, she could still hear it above and beyond the buzz of cicadas.

* * *

Kate groaned into her pillow and then remembered it was Sunday and Sundays were Sundays all over the world.

Perfect silence. Bliss.

If the pool was unoccupied she would swim, and then she would take a walk around the estate and generally try to unwind because everything was getting on top of her. Work was exhausting and trying to deal with these strange new feelings inside her was exhausting too. And she didn't need any of this, she told herself as she dressed in shorts and T-shirt over her bikini.

'Oh, Lorraine,' Kate breathed in surprise as she emerged from the house, expecting to see Guy sitting at the table under the shade in the courtyard. 'Where's Charo?' she asked.

Lorraine looked up from the magazine she was idly flicking through and gave her a mean look.

'The servants' whereabouts are no concern of mine,' she told Kate brittly, 'and before you ask where Guy is too I haven't any idea. He and Conrad drove off together and that is why I am here.'

Suddenly she slammed the magazine down on the table and stood up, all elegance in a linen outfit of white tapered trousers and safari shirt, with a leopard-print silk scarf draped at her pale throat, all rage with blue eyes as cold as glaciers.

'What I have to say to you is for your ears only, Kate Stephens,' she went on. 'Don't you *ever* set me up like that again! Don't you ever even think about it!'

Pale with shock, Kate widened her eyes and then the blood rushed back to her face. 'I don't know what you are talking about.'

'Don't know what I'm talking about!' Lorraine echoed furiously. 'You know *exactly* what I'm talking about! You stand there trying to look as innocent as a saint and—'

Kate spun away from her, following an instinctive urge to take flight from the enemy. She didn't know what Lorraine was trying to get at but whatever it was her fury terrified her. The coffee-pot was still warm on the hob and she snatched at it and shakily poured herself a cup and took a sip of it. To her horror she heard Lorraine behind her.

'But you're not as innocent as a saint, are you, Kate? You've known exactly what you were doing from day one with this company!'

Kate turned then and faced her, the caffeine giving her some strength. Her first thought was how very out of place Lorraine was in this rustic kitchen, and somehow now she understood what Guy had been getting at last night. She understood why she had been given this accommodation and not Lorraine. Lorraine was all glitz and admirably suited to her billeting in the lavish villa.

'Lorraine, will you please calm down and—?'

'And don't patronise me, Kate. I'm furious and I'll stay furious until I've told you exactly what I think of you!'

Kate sipped her coffee and leaned back against the sink, hoping she looked cool and composed although she wasn't inside.

'Go on,' she said levelly. 'Get it off your chest and then perhaps you'll give me a chance to state my case.'

Lorraine's eyes narrowed spitefully. 'So you do know what I'm getting at.'

'No, I don't,' Kate insisted, still calm. 'But you are furious for a reason and that reason is obviously something to do with me, and I've never given you reason to be mad at me so therefore I *must* have a case to state!'

'Oh, don't get tricky on me—'

'Do you want a coffee?' Kate interrupted, wondering just how long she could hold onto her temper.

'I wouldn't drink coffee in this dump, which just goes to show how far you would go to get your hands on Guy.'

So Guy was what it was all about. She'd wondered how long it would be before Lorraine challenged her over them both staying here.

'Guy put me in here because he thought I might appreciate it,' she murmured, knowing it was useless to try and explain any further. Guy was right. Most people associated Marbella with glitz, forgetting that it had once been a simple Andalusian fishing village before the developers got their hands on it.

'Guy put you in here to keep you out of *our* way,' Lorraine scathed. 'Just because you are sharing the same roof it doesn't mean to say your dreams are about to come true; far from it. I told you a long while back that Guy doesn't rise to challenges, he doesn't need to, so when your scheme didn't work you resorted to the big come-on.'

Kate's eyes widened. What was the 'big come-on' when it was at home?

Lorraine folded her arms across her chest. 'I bet you thought you'd cracked it when you found you were sharing this...this midden with him. So when exactly did you find out Guy wasn't rising to the bait?'

'What bait, Lorraine? I really don't know what you are trying to suggest.' Oh, this was awful, so embarrassing.

Lorraine shook her head and let out a snort of cynical laughter. 'The Kate Stephens' I'm-not-interested bait—that cool demeanour of yours, cultivated to bring men to heel and make them wonder why you're not like all the others.'

'I'm not like all the others,' Kate protested. 'I never have been interested in Guy or any other man in the company.'

'Oh, yeah! Pull the other one, Kate. Well, it didn't work with Guy and you must have been sick at that, and desperate too. So desperate, you did what you did.'

'And what did I do, Lorraine?' Kate sighed. She turned away to put her cup down and when she turned back to the already irate Lorraine she was alarmed at the poison in the girl's eyes.

'Still trying to play innocent! You really are the ultimate bitch, Kate. You know the situation between me and Guy and I'm not going to allow you to come between us. Guy isn't interested in you— never has been and never will be. I'm warning you, don't ever attempt to palm me off with Conrad again.'

'I never have!' Kate promised hotly. 'Just what the hell is going on here?'

For a split second Lorraine looked uncertain, but then the ice was back and her shoulders stiffened.

'You deliberately arranged that dinner last night with Guy and put him in a very embarrassing situation. He couldn't refuse your invitation when you had gone to such lengths. And then, just to make sure I was well out of the way, you obviously worked it so that Conrad invited me out.'

'Just a minute,' Kate blazed. Her head was reeling. It hadn't been like that at all. It had been Guy's idea to dine at the guest house. As for Conrad...did Lorraine really believe that she, Kate, had enough influence over him to persuade him to take her out to dinner? 'You're wrong, Lorraine, so very wrong.'

'I'm spot-on,' the other girl fired back at her. 'I'm not interested in Conrad. He's not half the man his brother is. He knows how Guy and I feel about each other but you must have said something to him because suddenly he is inviting me out to dinner. Last night was a nightmare for me, doubly so knowing what you were trying to do with Guy over your intimate little dinner.'

Her finger came up and she pointed it warningly at Kate. 'Don't ever try it again because you are way out of your league. Just remember why you were put in this dump—to keep you out of the way so Guy and I could get it together elsewhere without arousing suspicion with his brother. Now have I made myself clear?'

Dismayed and horrified, Kate couldn't raise another word of protest to her lips. She stared at Lorraine with wide eyes, wanting so desperately to protest her innocence but knowing it was useless. Lorraine would never believe it had been Guy's idea to dine here last night. Anger at Guy for putting her in this position pulsed deep inside her.

'Do I have to repeat myself?' Lorraine grated.

'No,' Kate murmured. 'Once is enough.'

And it would be. She was innocent of all charges but sadly only she knew it. She stood at the sink, motionless as Lorraine turned on her heel and strode out. She hadn't invited Guy to dine with her; he had invited her. She hadn't set Lorraine up with Conrad; she wasn't devious or desirous enough to do it. What she had done was to allow Guy Latham into her heart after bleating to herself about how much she disliked him. But that was a testament to the man's depth of persuasion; this feeling inside her was proof that she was falling under his spell.

And Lorraine, of all people, had been the one to bring it home to her because the one thing that had hurt above all Lorraine's wicked accusations was Guy's reason for putting her in this lovely old *finca*. To keep her out of the way so that he could carry on his affair with Lorraine without arousing suspicion.

Slowly she rinsed her cup under the tap. She must be some naïve idiot for not having seen that for herself. Do the opposite to avoid suspicion. Conrad would think it was she and Guy who were an item but that didn't take into account all the trips Guy took with Lorraine every afternoon.

Kate sighed. Who was playing games here she couldn't fathom. She *was* out of her league with these sophisticates of amorous intrigue. Perhaps she should have involved herself more in the office gossip. She might have learned a few helpful techniques in dealing with it. Instead she was floundering, not even able to rationalise what was happening inside her, this strange new feeling for Guy. . .

*   *   *

'Those errors in the figures last week—why didn't you tell me they were Lorraine's mistakes, not yours?' Guy stormed as he came into the office after coffee on Monday morning.

Kate glared at him across the office. How on earth had he found out? Surely Lorraine hadn't admitted her guilt, especially not after her furious accusations yesterday?

'I don't tell tales,' she told him quietly, realising that was an admission in itself.

He came and stood over her, dark and menacing. How he had found out Kate didn't ask. He'd been in a private meeting with his brother most of the morning and she supposed it had come up then.

'In company matters you do tell tales, Kate. You saw discrepancies, took the blame for them yourself and endured my wrath and never said a word in defence of yourself. How am I expected to look on that when it comes to viewing you for promotion?'

Kate stood up from her computer to face him. This was the last straw. Whatever she did wasn't right.

'It wasn't that important,' she reasoned.

'It could have been.'

'But it wasn't! Lorraine made a couple of errors—'

'And you covered for her. That is not what is expected of Latham employees, Kate. Your allegiance is to me and the company and you should have pointed out that Lorraine was at fault and not yourself.'

'Well, in any other circumstances I would have done!' Kate retorted.

'What other circumstances?' he growled.

'The emotional circumstances,' Kate said bravely. 'You talk of company allegiance but you can't have it all, you know. Would you have believed me if I'd told you Lorraine wasn't doing her job properly?'

'Why shouldn't I?' he questioned, broad shoulders going up.

'Because you are romantically involved with her, that's why. Instead of accusing me of every discrepancy in the world, give *her* a dressing down next time you're thrashing around between the corporate sheets!'

She spun away from him, regretting her outburst as usual, wishing she had as much control of her mouth as she had over her emotions—which was a contradictory thought as her emotions were all over the place at the moment.

He caught her arm and spun her back round and she expected anger from him, but he surprised her by being cool and calm.

'Lorraine and I do not thrash around between any sort of sheets, and even if you think so it is no reason to hold back on—'

'It's every reason, Guy,' she argued. 'You run your business like a house of ill repute and yet you expect efficiency and—'

His eyes blackened and his grip on her upper arm tightened. 'And you, sweetheart, are walking the tightrope again. Tread carefully. Any more of that and you're fired!'

The warning registered loud and clear and the injustice of it all fanned her anger till it was white-hot. Because of everything—her funny feelings, Lorraine's warnings, his accusations—she knew she couldn't stand any more. She wrenched herself out of his grasp.

'I'll save you the trouble. I'm firing myself—out of here and as far away from you and your tricky games as possible. I do my work well but it isn't enough. You expect too much.'

She stormed out of the room, angry and bitter and burning with one awful thought over all others. So now she was jobless, but she really didn't care because worst of all was that after today she wouldn't see Guy Latham ever again and, dammit, that really mattered.

CHAPTER SIX

GUY caught up with Kate in the gardens, exactly
on the spot where he had first taken her in his arms
and kissed her, only to accuse her of taking the in-
itiative. The first injustice, and a multitude had
followed since.

He swung her around and she cried out as his
fingers bit brutally into her upper arm again.

'Let me go! I'll be black and blue before you
finish with me!'

'The way you are going you'll be lucky to get
away with your life,' he warned furiously. 'You
don't walk out on me—'

'I didn't walk out on you! I walked out on the
company—this stinking company that doesn't know
where to draw the line between business and lust.
You expect working standards in a hotbed environment and it just doesn't work. You're having
an affair with the other member of staff on this
assignment and you can't see the predicament that
puts me in, thrust between the passionate crossfire!'

He let out a sigh of exasperation and turned her
to the arched door. Kicking it open, he pushed her
into the courtyard and marched her into the house,
calling for Charo. She answered from the kitchen
and Guy let Kate go to stride across the terracotta-
tiled floor.

Kate seized her chance for escape and flew upstairs to her bedroom. She was going and he wasn't

going to stop her. She couldn't stay because she was hurting too deeply. *He* was hurting her, Lorraine was hurting her and worst of all she was hurting herself by allowing these wretched feelings inside her to matter. She was hurling clothes into her suitcase when he walked in.

'What are you doing?' he grated.

Mute, Kate raised her eyes skywards and carried on packing.

'You are being absurd, Kate.'

'So I'm being absurd. It's my life so therefore my privilege.'

He closed a very firm hand over hers and with the other snatched a blouse from her fingers and tossed it across the bed. None too gently he pushed her down on the edge of the mattress, tipped out the contents of the case beside her and firmly deposited it against the wall.

'You have no privileges while you are here working for me,' he told her as he came back and stood over her. 'And you don't walk out on the job leaving me floundering for a new assistant. You're not leaving unless I see fit to let you go. Do you understand?'

'Do *you* understand that I've just quit?' Kate retaliated hotly, wishing he weren't standing so close over her because she wanted to be on her feet to face him and there just wasn't room. 'I'm going because I can't take any more. You just threatened to fire me,' Kate went on grimly. 'Totally unjustified, too. A few home truths that you can't face and you are ready to fire me.'

'If they were home truths I wouldn't have made the threat. You've blown this out of all proportion.

I am not emotionally involved with Lorraine and never have been.'

She stared up at him and steeled her heart against him. She believed him because you didn't have to be emotionally involved to be bedding someone! She wondered how poor Lorraine would feel if she could hear him now, coldly denying that he had any feelings for her and yet using her the way he was. She hated him for deceiving Lorraine so; she hated him for what he was doing to her, too, swinging her emotions till she was dizzy with uncertainty.

'It makes no difference now. I still want to leave.' She stood up then, expecting him to move aside for her, but he didn't. He stood his ground and she faced him, so close, they were almost touching. 'And I will,' she pronounced firmly, eyes narrowed to add more defiance to her statement.

His eyes darkened, his jawline tensed and he spoke through gritted teeth. 'Don't fight me, Kate, because you'll come off the worst, I promise you. You criticise the way I run this company but you are the only one complaining. It all runs extremely smoothly, thanks to me. My methods might not be to your liking but they work, and you won't work if you walk out on Latham's at this moment in time.'

Kate drew in her breath and her eyes blazed. 'Is that a threat to my future?'

'Take it how you will,' he said dangerously.

Kate took it the way he meant it—that he would withhold references and block any new career move she might attempt after leaving his company. She was on to a loser and recognised it. Before this trip she hadn't realised just how much power he wielded, but now, after working with him so closely, she knew that it far outweighed the power she had thought his brother had. She knew his contacts in similar business set-ups and she wouldn't stand a chance if she applied to them for a job. Though she hated to admit it, Guy Latham was some powerful man in his field.

'So I can't leave,' she murmured humbly.

'No, you can't leave, Kate.'

'Not ever?'

He gripped her arms and she tried not to freeze against him and show how much he unnerved her, but the reaction was instinctive. He felt her tensing and his eyes narrowed.

'Back in the UK you will probably have to, one way or the other,' he said enigmatically.

She flashed her dark eyes at him. 'And what is that supposed to mean?'

'You'll find out. Now, shall we forget all this quitting business?'

He was still gripping her arms but the timbre of his voice had changed and she wondered what on earth he meant by that strange remark of his. But she had pushed him, she supposed, and once away from Spain she doubted she'd get away with being so outspoken with him. On her return to London he would very likely sack her on the spot, but not now; now he needed her because Lorraine certainly couldn't handle the workload on her own.

'On one condition.' She rallied, defiant to the end. 'I get some freedom from now on. Some of the freedom Lorraine is allowed. I'm like a prisoner here and—'

'You are here to work, Kate,' he told her, tightening his hold on her just as she was about to pull away. 'This isn't your summer vacation.'

'I wasn't aiming to go sunning myself on some beach, you know,' she argued. 'Most days you go off with Lorraine, shopping, and—'

'That's business, not pleasure.'

'Huh! Funny business, if you ask me.'

'I'm not asking you.'

'Well, I'm telling you how I feel when I see you both coming back from your trips, laughing and looking as if you've been having fun and her loaded up with packages and—'

'My, you don't miss much, do you?'

'No, I don't. I don't miss anything!' she sparked meaningfully.

'And you're jealous?'

His tone was loaded with mockery, as if he had caught her out. Kate blazed inside to think that he just might know how she was feeling.

'Yes, I am jealous,' she responded hotly, and shook her arms free of him then and turned away to her bundle of clothes on the bed, sweeping them up into her arms. 'Not of Lorraine in the way you think, but because I'd like to go out and shop till I drop. One rule for her and another for me and you have the nerve to deny any emotional involvement with her!' Fury powered her across the room to the wardrobe where she scrabbled around trying to get blouses on hangers without dropping them.

He came over to her, scooped the lot from her arms, threw them into the wardrobe and slammed the door shut. He swung her to face him yet again, his eyes holding hers with some strange look that sent a shiver down her spine. She tensed herself back against the wardrobe.

'I take Lorraine out to visit clients because Conrad wants her down here in Spain permanently, but that information is between you, me and my brother at the moment. Any shopping she does *en route* is incidental. This isn't a fun trip, this is hard work. I've told you why I want you here when I'm not and as my employee you should understand that.'

But Kate didn't understand it—none of it. Conrad wanted Lorraine down here all the time? Well, Lorraine didn't know that. And when she did know how would she feel, hating Conrad so? And if she and Guy were such an *item* why was Guy going along with this?

'We've been through all this before,' Kate argued, not wanting to dwell on Lorraine and Conrad when her own affairs were so dominant and demanding attention. 'But it doesn't get any better, it gets worse. This is a business trip, yes, you keep reminding me and I understand, but it hasn't stopped you—'

She didn't finish because he leaned his head down to hers and panic seized her, her heart and her pulses racing because she knew just what he was going to do.

'And it won't stop me this time,' he breathed heatedly against her face. His mouth came to hers and she couldn't pull away because the awful thing was that she didn't want to. His lips were on hers, so warm and sensual, imprisoning her in a world she knew so little about. Sensuality gave way to passion and she knew the dangers, yet couldn't resist because he drew all her strength from her. Shame burned within her for what she was allowing: his sexual power to overcome her.

He pressed hard against her, melding his body with hers, claiming her wholly and completely. She felt the hard wooden wardrobe door against her back and it was the only reality; the rest was the stuff of fantasy. Guy kissing her, Guy's heat against her body, his male scent spinning her senses, trapping her in a vacuum she wanted no escape from. She knew in that moment of desire and crushing pleasure that she wanted him to go on and on, to keep up the passion till there was no going back.

And he knew and it spurred him to ease his hand up from her waist to smooth it over her breast. His mouth hardened against hers as if the warmth of her taut breast under his touch was firing a new urgency in him. With that new urgency he pulled her blouse loose from her skirt and his touch on her naked flesh made her stiffen against him, shocking her with the intense need it aroused in her.

She murmured a vague 'No' against his lips, but it was too vague to make any impression. His hand cupped her breast, grazing heatedly over her bra, and then his fingers made contact with the naked swell of flesh above the lace. Shakily she drew back from him then, pressed her palms to his chest, and this time her cry of protest could be heard.

'Please don't.'

She couldn't look at him, couldn't raise her lowered eyes to meet his. He drew back slightly and lifted her chin and she squeezed her eyes shut.

'Open your eyes, Kate, and look at me,' he ordered, his voice thick, his other hand still smoothing the burning skin above her bra.

She obeyed. Biting her lip, she slowly blinked open her eyes and gradually raised them up from his mouth, his nose, to his dark eyes.

'What you see is my desire. What I see is yours. So now we both know, don't we?' he challenged in a very low voice.

Kate bit harder on her lip and stared at him with wide, misty eyes. He could see so much but still he was blind. She could see beyond this momentary desire and knew what the future would hold if she gave in to him—the same as her future with Gustav had once held: heartache and loss. Everything her mother had taught her to expect.

She shook her head, shaking her chin free from his touch. 'It means nothing,' she whispered, and brought her hand up to draw his away from her breast. His fingers coiled around hers and he held her.

His eyes darkened. 'It means everything. Don't try and play the innocent with me any more. Don't argue with me any more either, because by fighting me you are showing just how much you want me.'

Kate flared at his unreasonableness. 'But you don't want me!' she protested. 'You put it very succinctly just then. Desire, you said—well, I'm not into desire. I'm just a challenge to you because I'm not like the others, willing to fall into your arms at the slightest provocation.'

'You just did,' he informed her knowingly.

She pushed him away and stumbled to the middle of the room and then turned on him, eyes wide and blazing.

'You had me forced up against an unyielding door, Guy Latham. I had no choice but to suffer you.'

'You had every choice, sweetheart. I don't push my attentions where they are not wanted.'

'You just did,' she insisted, and knew she was getting precisely nowhere with him. He was a master of seduction because he'd had enough practice and practice made perfect. 'Get out of my bedroom,' she cried.

He stepped towards her again. 'Don't order me out of my own room, Kate. In fact, don't order me to do anything other than join you on that bed.'

'What bed?'

She squealed as the backs of her legs made contact with the hard wooden edge of the bed, un-balancing her and tipping her backwards onto the soft mattress.

Suddenly he was bending over her, one hand steadying himself on the lacy cover, the other cupping her trembling chin.

'It's going to happen, you know. You and me in this bed, some time soon. The quicker you accept it and stop playing your silly virtuous games, the better it will be for both of us. I hope I make myself clear because I wouldn't like to have to go through this charade again.'

Kate gritted her teeth. 'That's just what it is to you—a guessing game with all the relevant actions; trouble is, you keep getting it wrong. Well, let me spell it out to you, Guy. You are not bedding me in this bed or any other. I don't fool around with just anybody and you are just anybody!'

She expected him to be angry because it was her intention to make him so, but he just laughed in her face. 'No, you only fool around with men old enough to be your father, and perhaps that is what I find so fascinating about you. Or maybe I just want to prove to you what a little fool you are. Maybe I do see you as a challenge—as you obviously believe. But what fun I'm going to have discovering the real you.'

He released her chin and grinned down at her and then he turned away and was gone. In fury she grasped the first thing to hand—a blouse he had snatched from her—and balled it and hurled it at the door, and it was a very feeble attempt to have the last fling at him.

Later she uncoiled herself from the bed and went to the window for air, but there was less outside than in. She wanted to swim but how could she? He might be there.

She felt more and more the prisoner he was making her. Soon she wouldn't be able to step out of this room for fear of him. And now she really did fear him because he made her feel so weak and vulnerable and he knew the power he had over her. She couldn't even anger him any more; he'd gone beyond that stage. She was a challenge and a figure of fun to him and she minded so much that it hurt, badly. Knowing it all, knowing what fired him and hating him for it, she still felt inexplicably hurt by it.

*   *   *

Kate was very quiet at dinner that night. It was another test of endurance as they all gathered around the long table on the terrace at the villa. It was exceptionally hot, without a breath of air to alleviate the oppressive atmosphere.

Kate watched them all. Conrad was quieter than usual. Lorraine was striving for conversation with Guy, as if she could sense him slipping out of her reach, Guy smiling and acknowledging her presence—but only just.

It troubled Kate to see Lorraine this way and Guy so cool with her. If what Lorraine had implied was true and she and Guy were heavily into a relationship, surely they wouldn't be able to conceal it? Guy had denied it and, watching him now, Kate believed his denial. Or was there behaviour just a cover-up for Conrad's benefit, as Lorraine had suggested the bedding arrangements were?

'You haven't touched your wine, Kate,' Guy said. 'Not to your taste?'

Kate lifted her glass. 'It's excellent.'

'Would you know if it wasn't?' Lorraine put in spitefully.

'Probably not,' Kate returned, the irritating heat of the night prompting a quick response from her. 'I'm not a wine buff, but I'm sure Conrad wouldn't tolerate an inferior wine at his table so I presume it is excellent.'

Lorraine glowered at her and Conrad laughed. 'Very diplomatic of you, Kate.' He proceeded to launch into a detailed account of his wine-buying trips to the Penedes region of Spain and Kate felt a yawn coming on but suppressed it.

Later they adjourned inside the villa for coffee and brandy because the heat outside was so oppressive. Air-conditioning cooled the softly lit, marble-floored sitting room with its white leather sofas and glass-topped tables edged with gilt. White leather and gilt were in abundance everywhere. It was the first time Kate had seen the interior, apart from the office suite at the rear, and it wasn't to her taste, and she wondered how Guy could have known her taste when he had offered her the lovely rustic guest house.

Lorraine was perfectly at home here, Kate noticed as she seated herself on one of the long sofas. She watched as Lorraine crossed to the hi-fi in her gilt-heeled sandals and selected a CD and loaded it. Soft, smoochy music came at her from all corners and Kate squirmed as Lorraine turned to Guy, endowed him with a beguiling smile and held her arms out to him in a silent invitation to dance. As Guy had his back to Kate she couldn't see his facial reaction but as he stepped towards Lorraine and folded her against him it could hardly be construed as a refusal.

Kate's heart thudded painfully as she watched them move languidly in time to the music, Guy smiling down at the lovely Lorraine and the lovely Lorraine smiling up at him as if all her dreams were about to land at her feet, gift-wrapped.

'They make a very attractive couple, don't they?' Conrad said as he handed Kate a brandy and sat down beside her.

'Yes, they do,' Kate agreed, her hand tightening around the bowl of the goblet.

'Very ill-suited, though, but Lorraine doesn't know that yet and Guy likes playing with fire, as you probably know.'

Mystified, Kate stared into her goblet. She really didn't understand these people. They were all playing games.

'So tell me, how did you enjoy the dinner Guy laid on for you the other night?'

So it *had* been Guy's idea. Kate felt no joy at knowing for sure because the reason was obvious now. He'd had seduction in mind but it had come to nothing because she hadn't given him the right opening. Biding his time, no doubt.

'It was very nice. Charo is a very good cook.' Kate raised her eyes to see Lorraine wrapping her arms even tighter around Guy. He was responding, too, his hands around her tiny waist, scarcely a hair's breadth between them, cheek to cheek now. Kate fought the feeling of jealousy coiling inside her. How could she be jealous when she despised him so? How confusing life was.

'H-how was your evening out with Lorraine?' Kate forced herself to speak. She turned her head towards Conrad and in that moment saw a look in his eye that she didn't understand. He was watching the two dancers, eyes dark and cold, and Kate felt a thread of wariness run through her. She didn't know Conrad well enough to interpret that look, but it certainly wasn't one of pleasure.

Suddenly he turned to her and gave her his full attention. 'Very nice, yes, very nice, but, you know, it made me feel a little guilty. Guy has worked you so hard and you haven't been out at all yourself. You work equally hard as Lorraine.' He reached out and patted her knee and smiled at her. 'I aim to put that to rights. Tomorrow.'

Kate laughed hesitantly. Surely he didn't mean to ask her out? To compensate her for the drudgery Guy was inflicting on her?

'Tomorrow afternoon we'll take a little trip of our own, a treat for us both. I know a very nice French restaurant in Puerto Banus and—'

'That isn't necessary, Conrad,' Kate said quietly, her eyes still on Lorraine and Guy. They were in a world of their own, moving only very slightly in a tiny circle to the low, moody music. Lorraine was whispering something in Guy's ear, probably the words to the romantic melody, Kate mused despondently.

'If they are not careful they'll screw themselves into the ground,' Conrad said under his breath, and his choice of words brought a very small smile to Kate's lips. 'I doubt we'll be missed tomorrow and if we are it can only be to the good,' Conrad went on, in such a low voice that Kate wondered if she had heard him right.

'We'll leave before lunch.'

'Conrad,' Kate breathed, 'you don't have to—'

'I want to, Kate,' Conrad insisted, and patted her knee again. Kate wished he wouldn't do that. 'You deserve a treat for all the work you have put in. I appreciate you even if Guy doesn't. Now I'll hear no more of it. Two o'clock tomorrow.' He stood up and moved away to the bar to get another drink and Kate lifted her brandy to her lips and took a huge gulp.

She didn't want to go out with Conrad tomorrow and yet last week she would have been thrilled at the thought. She hated sitting here watching Guy and Lorraine making an exhibition of themselves yet last week she wouldn't have cared. So much had changed in such a short space of time that it made her query her sanity. She drained her brandy goblet, set it down on the table next to her and got to her feet. She couldn't bear any more.

'Not so fast.' Guy caught her arm as she was about to step out onto the terrace. 'Where are you off to in such a hurry?'

'Bed,' she seethed under her breath for fear of being overheard, though a quick glance over his shoulder to see Conrad persuading a reluctant Lorraine into his arms assured her that she wouldn't be heard by them. '*On my own*,' she emphasised, 'so don't get any foolish ideas.'

'I don't have any foolish ideas where you are concerned, Kate. They are all rational. I'll wait to be invited but don't think you are home and dry. I'll push for that invite in my own way. Now, before you go at least give me a sporting chance.'

'What have you got in mind—a fifty-yard start?' she taunted sarcastically, and wrenched away from him. She got nowhere. He grasped at her again, this time swinging her back into the villa where Conrad and Lorraine were locked together in the middle of the room. Before she knew it Guy had drawn her into his arms to move sensually with the music.

'I don't want to dance with you, Guy,' she hissed through thinned lips, 'so unhand me.'

He held her so tightly that she hadn't a chance of escape without causing a scene.

'Why should I when I'm just warmed up?'

'And it was plain for everyone to see who warmed you up.'

'Ah, I might whet my appetite outside but I always eat at home, and you know where I lay my head at night,' he breathed into her ear.

'You are impossible!'

'And so are you. Don't you know how to dance?' He grasped her arm and moved it around his back. 'There, isn't that better?'

'No, it is not. I don't want to do this!'

'Relax, sunshine. It's really very nice.'

His hands held her so strongly that she knew it was useless to struggle. Her own hands were stiff and unyielding across his back and she hoped Lorraine could see that she wasn't enjoying this one bit.

Gradually Guy relaxed his hold on her, but the way he smoothed his hands across her back and then down to her hips made Kate tense even more. His body heat merged with hers till she felt faint. The side of his cheek was against hers and Kate closed her eyes, but not with pleasure. It was painful being in his arms, knowing he was thrusting temptation at her, knowing she was just a game to him. For a moment she wished it weren't this way, wished he truly wanted her and that they were a couple in love. Was she falling in love with him? How could she be when he angered her so?

She felt his hand leave her back and smooth down the side of her face, almost a loving caress, as if he truly cared. She blinked open her eyes and he was looking down at her and smiling such a mysterious smile.

'You are easily the most beautiful woman in the room,' he whispered softly

Kate's heart thudded at his nerve. Only minutes ago he had probably said the very same thing to Lorraine. Her eyes must have spoken her thoughts because he added, 'And I haven't told anyone else that tonight.'

Before she could respond he kissed her softly parted lips, so tenderly that she might have believed he meant it. For a few ecstatic seconds she yielded to the pull of his magnetism and let her fantasies go wild. She imagined going further than this kiss, letting herself be led by him wherever he wanted to take her, through the gates of sensuality and way beyond. Guy loving her, leading her, taking her, making her feel so complete that all her mistrust and doubt would be swept away on the tidal wave of his passion and need for her.

The kiss deepened as if he too was on that fantasy voyage with her, and as he moved his hips against hers, tempting her to go with him wherever he willed, Kate suddenly saw the risk he was taking by kissing her so openly and suggestively in full view of Conrad and Lorraine. She pulled back, hot and embarrassed, and tried to jerk herself out of his arms, but he held onto her and looked deep into her eyes.

He spoke in a whisper. 'There's no one here, Kate, just you and me.'

Wide-eyed, Kate spun out of his arms and this time he let her go. Her eyes searched the room, not believing. No one. In confusion she turned back to Guy. He was smiling at her, that strange smile of his that gave nothing away.

'So now you know,' he said smoothly.

Kate stared at him hard, not knowing anything, only that the music was still playing softly in the background and the cicadas were still clicking away on the terrace outside. There was no sign of Conrad or Lorraine and she hadn't heard them leave. Where were they anyway?

Slowly, very slowly, a light dawned.

She shook her head, not believing it possible. 'No,' she uttered weakly. 'She ... Lorraine ... she doesn't ... doesn't like him.'

Guy's enigmatic smile widened and he shrugged slightly and his softly spoken words were nevertheless loaded with meaning. 'That's women for you.'

Blood rushed to her head and she felt slightly faint. Was this the game women played, denying their attraction to a certain man to cover their real feelings? But no, Lorraine had been adamant. She didn't want to know Conrad. But then ... but then Kate had once hated Guy. Only days ago she had loathed him and now ... and now she was more confused than ever.

She stepped back from Guy, truly afraid because she really didn't know what was happening to everyone. Hot, balmy Mediterranean nights. Lorraine and Conrad. She and Guy.

She steeled herself inside, valiantly fought her faintness and lifted her chin. 'Goodnight, Guy,' she said softly.

His response was the last she expected from him. 'Goodnight, Kate. Sleep well.'

In a daze she found her way back to the guest house. In a daze she slid into bed and, still dazed, a long while later she heard his bedroom door close after him and then an eerie silence. Sleep well? There wasn't the remotest chance of that as she lay through the hot night trying to understand exactly what had happened tonight. ·

CHAPTER SEVEN

'LORRAINE—'

'Not now, Kate,' Lorraine said snappily with a frown on her brow. She tossed a wad of faxes onto Kate's desk and turned away.

'It won't take a minute,' Kate pleaded. She had to talk to her, somehow try and break through the ice between them. She needed to know what was going on, why everyone was acting the way they were. She hadn't seen Guy all morning but she would have got nothing from him anyway. He lived in his own world of mystery and intrigue.

'A minute I haven't got,' Lorraine retorted dismissively. She turned at the door and gave Kate a very sweet smile. 'Guy and I are taking a drive up to a little town in the hills. The real Spain, apparently. *Hasta luego*,' she sang, and slammed the door after her.

Kate sat stiffly at her console. So now Guy was giving Lorraine the 'real Spain' treatment. He was obviously weary of trying to impress *her* with it.

'We'll go a little earlier than two, Kate,' Conrad said from the door, so unexpectedly that Kate jumped and went hot. 'In fact—' he glanced at his watch '—now would suit me fine.'

Kate glanced at her own watch with a frown. How could she tell Conrad she'd rather go out on her own? In fact, when it came down to it, she didn't feel much like going on her own either. What

127

she really wanted to do was get this assignment finished, get back to the UK and pretend none of it had happened.

'Conrad, it isn't necessary for you to come with me—'

'I don't break my word, Kate.' He smiled. 'I promised you a treat. I'll meet you at the front in ten minutes.'

It was too late to protest. Conrad had gone. Kate stood by the patio doors, gazing out at the vibrant geraniums in their terracotta pots. How everything had changed. Once she would have been thrilled at the thought of Conrad taking her out. Now he left her cold. He wasn't the man she had imagined him to be in her fantasies. At times he seemed much older than his years and just now had spoken to her as if she were a daughter he couldn't break a promise to.

If Guy had been taking her out her heart would have been racing. She rubbed her forehead as if trying to rub him out of her life. They sparked off each other and yet he wanted her and she couldn't deny that she wanted him. It would be easy to succumb, but impossible. Her judgement of men wasn't exactly rock-solid, what with Gustav, with his wandering eye, Conrad, a misplaced romantic fantasy, and Guy, the man she had most loathed in the world, now setting her heart on fire. How fickle could she get?

Kate turned as Guy came into the office in a hurry to pick up some paperwork from his desk.

'That call from Roederers in Germany is expected this afternoon, Kate. Make sure you have the mobile with you.'

She stepped towards him, to tell him that Conrad was taking her out for the afternoon.

'Guy, I have to—'

'I shall phone them later, of course, but they are calling with some preliminary costings this afternoon, so make sure you get them right.'

He hadn't even heard. She sighed in resignation. She wanted an excuse not to go out with Conrad and Guy had handed her one.

'I always get them right,' she reminded him stiffly.

He stopped shuffling through the papers and looked at her, eyes glinting with impatience. 'It was just a reminder, Kate. Don't jump down my throat.'

'I didn't,' Kate protested. 'You are the one jumping down throats—mine. You don't have to tell me my duties.'

His eyes darkened threateningly. 'I was emphasising them, not telling you them. That call is of vital importance. We aren't the only ones pitching for the deal and a swift decision is essential.' He discarded some of the papers and slid the others into a plastic sheaf.

'If it's so important why don't you see to it yourself?' she deliberately taunted. She knew he was rushing around because he had a date with Lorraine. The thought burned.

'Because I have other things to attend to,' he told her, daring her to question what. He threw her a last steely look and went to the door, slamming it behind him.

Kate let out a sigh and went to her desk and picked up the mobile phone. And the 'other things to attend to' was Lorraine, and yet she was expected to sit around waiting for a call from Germany that might not come. But she would have to because he had emphasised the importance of it and the company came before pleasure. Besides, it was the perfect excuse to get out of her date with Conrad.

'Oh,' Kate gasped, stepping down into the sitting room after changing into a cool white sundress. 'I was just coming to tell you—'

Conrad was standing in the terracotta-floored sitting room, gazing around him in disapproval. 'I never know what Guy sees in this place. It's so dim and antiquated. Ah, you're ready,' he said more cheerfully, giving her his full attention. 'And very lovely too.'

'Conrad, I can't come. Guy needs me here to take a call from Roederers,' she explained.

'Roederers? Nonsense.' He laughed. 'They aren't due to call till tomorrow. It's just his little excuse to keep you under his thumb.' He picked up her bag from the sofa, gave it to her and took her arm. 'Come on, forget work, Kate,' he said cheerily. 'We promised ourselves a break and that is what we are going to have.'

Kate hesitantly pulled back. 'Guy said it was important, Conrad, and—' She stopped, seeing Conrad's eyes darken.

'You do as I say, Kate,' he said suddenly, so coldly that Kate felt the chill. 'You answer to me, not my brother. Forget the call; it's not important.'

Kate was still inwardly protesting the importance of the call as she reluctantly followed Conrad out of the house. Guy didn't make mistakes but maybe this time he had. Conrad had sounded so certain and . . . and wasn't he rushing her a bit? She had to hurry to keep up with him and why on earth had his tone changed so abruptly, so impatiently?

To Kate's astonishment Conrad linked his arm around her shoulders as they walked towards a silver Mercedes, the twin of Guy's white one, parked at the front of the villa. Lorraine was sitting in the shade on the terrace, obviously waiting for Guy. At sight of Conrad Kate noticed her uncross her legs and stiffen in her chair. Conrad suddenly laughed at nothing and leaned so close to Kate as he opened the passenger door for her that it must have looked as if they were lovers sharing a private joke.

Kate went cold. Naïve she had certainly been at the beginning of this trip but she was learning fast. She knew exactly what was going on. Conrad was acting way over the top with his false *bonhomie*, and all for Lorraine's benefit—to make her jealous.

Kate was sure of it as she watched Conrad's eyes as he started the engine. He was more intent on watching Lorraine's reaction than on watching where he was going, and they nearly hit a palm tree as Conrad reversed the car and then sped down the pink gravel driveway.

Dumbstruck, Kate could do nothing but tighten her seat belt and stare stoically ahead, wishing she'd been strong enough to refuse this outing and wishing she had remembered to bring the mobile phone with her. If that phone call came through and she missed it . . .

'But I insist, Kate. You must take full advantage of the time while we are here. Let me help you choose something. I've always prided myself on my good taste.'

Heaven forbid, Kate thought miserably as Conrad propelled her into an exclusive boutique in a small plaza of likewise exclusive boutiques. Lunch had been an awful affair, with Conrad drinking and talking too much, the subject Lorraine. And then he had insisted on taking her shopping and Kate was hating the whole afternoon and wishing with all her heart that Guy would come along and rescue her from his dreadful brother.

But there wasn't a hope. Guy was out with Lorraine, high up in the hills, and having a good deal better time than she was having. The thought made her so miserable that she wanted to cry.

'Carina, darling,' Conrad directed at the glamorous sales assistant, kissing her on both cheeks. 'Show dear Kate the very best and whatever she wants charge it to me.' He slumped down into the nearest chair, his face flushed and as creased as his linen trousers.

Obviously he wasn't a stranger here, Kate pondered, irritated that he had offered to pay for any purchases. But he was to be pitied more than anything, she supposed. He was in love with Lorraine and she wouldn't wish that on any man.

'O, I 'ave zee many beautiful theengs for you, *señorita*,' Carina crooned. 'You are zee most perfect size and eet will be my pleasure—'

'I'll take this,' Kate said quickly, seeing through her phony accent immediately. She pulled a peacock-blue silk cocktail dress from a rack and shoved it at the bronzed sales assistant, who looked astonished.

'You try eet on, *sí*?'

'I don't 'ave to,' Kate mimicked. 'I can zee eet will fit.'

As Carina widened her eyes with surprise, Kate took a furtive glance at Conrad, who was lolling in the chair, nearly dropping off to sleep. She stepped closer to the assistant and lowered her voice and said firmly, 'And I'll pay for it myself, and if you want the sale you let him think he's paid for it because frankly I've had all I can take from him this afternoon. All I want from now on is a quiet life.'

Carina grinned, dropping her accent. 'Listen, love. I don't care who pays for it. I'm on commission, whoever.'

Kate laughed. 'Where are you from?' she asked as Carina folded the dress and packaged it in tissue-paper and a huge glossy carrier.

Carina leaned towards her and whispered, 'Finchley; would you guess?'

Carina was the only bright spot in her afternoon. Kate laughed. 'Never in zee month of Sundays!'

While she processed Kate's credit card Carina confessed, 'An accent goes a long way down here. Nothing is real in Marbella—not to the likes of me, anyway.'

Not to the likes of me either, Kate inwardly agreed. Since she'd come here insanity had ruled over reality. The hot Mediterranean sun made madness compulsory.

'Anyway, what's a nice girl like you doing with Conrad Latham? He usually goes for blondes.'

That didn't surprise Kate, not now. Guy had warned her and she hadn't listened. She'd been wrong about Conrad and very wrong about Guy too. Her heart pulled at the hard time she had given him.

'He's my boss,' Kate told her. 'He and his brother are partners and his brother is everything he's not. Guy wouldn't be sitting there nodding off with drink, insulting me by trying to buy my clothes.' She felt herself blushing at what she was saying—actually flattering Guy. He hadn't been out of her thoughts all afternoon. A hundred times she had wished he had been with her, instead of Conrad.

'Got the wrong brother, have you?' Carina said as she slipped the bill into the glossy carrier and handed Kate her card back.

Kate looked at her and gave a small smile. 'No, I've got the right one,' she said softly, and touched her heart. She knew then that Guy meant far more to her than any man ever had before, and she knew, after this awful afternoon with his brother, that she was going to try and change. She was going to stop fighting him, for one thing.

'Are you going to wake him or shall I?' Carina whispered to Kate as they both stood in front of a lolling, sleeping Conrad.

'Have this one on me.' Kate grinned.

'Oh, Señor Latham,' Carina enthused loudly, clasping her hands together with ecstasy. Conrad blinked open his eyes. 'Zee dress your daughter choose ees so beautiful. She 'as good taste like 'er *Papa*. You bring 'er again, sí?'

Kate was still laughing, albeit inwardly, when they got back to the car. Poor Conrad, he still looked flushed and affronted that someone could have mistaken her for his daughter.

'I'll drive, Conrad,' she told him by the car, holding out her hand for the keys. She'd been worried about getting back to the villa since Conrad had started drinking in the restaurant.

'I'm quite capable,' he protested huffily.

He wasn't capable at all. 'I know you are—' Kate smiled at him endearingly '—but, well, you've been so sweet to me today and I hate to ask for more but... I've never driven a Mercedes before and... Oh, please, Conrad, let me drive it home.'

Her eyes were wide and appealing, her pink lips slightly apart in expectation; how could he refuse her? Kate let out a squeal of delight and clapped her hands like a child as Conrad grinned and tossed her the keys.

''Struth, I'll never go to heaven,' she muttered under her breath as she slid into the driver's seat.

'You know, Lorraine is such a smart lady but—'

'Seat belt,' Kate interrupted to warn him. Please shut up and belt up at the same time, Kate prayed. She'd heard enough about Lorraine to last her a lifetime.

'Yes, yes,' he mumbled, and fumbled with his belt. 'You'd think she'd know how she felt by now. All this dithering and playing hard to get...'

Kate concentrated on the build-up of traffic down on the coast road. The tarmac shimmered in the glaring heat and drivers were irritable and honking their horns and Kate longed to be back in the cool guest house with a long iced drink. She hoped Guy would be back and his trip with Lorraine had been business and not pleasure and they could talk and... and sort of start all over again.

'Oh, hell!' Kate cursed, braking sharply as the car in front braked. A crescendo of car horns rose up into the dry, dusty air and then suddenly the Mercedes was shunted violently from behind and Kate jerked forward, the seat belt jarring across her chest but saving her forehead from the windscreen.

Conrad shot forward, though, and caught his head on the rear-view mirror then jerked back like a rag doll, his head thudding on the headrest.

'Conrad!' Kate cried leaning across him. 'Are you all right?' She saw that he hadn't fastened his seat belt. It lay limp across his lap.

'What the hell...?' he said in a daze, and fumbled at the passenger door. 'Damned tourists!'

Kate caught his arm and pulled him back and lashed his seat belt across him. The last thing she wanted was him out on the highway, drunkenly making the situation ten times worse.

'I'll deal with it,' she insisted, buckling him up. 'You've been drinking and you didn't have your belt clipped.'

To her amazement he stayed still, and Kate got out and faced a very red-faced Spaniard who'd driven a dilapidated vegetable lorry into the back of the Mercedes.

A cast of thousands—or so it seemed—appeared, gesticulating wildly and, thankfully, on Kate's side. It was an hour before they were able to leave after the formalities, which Kate handled with a serenity that even surprised herself. After the dreadful afternoon with the moribund Conrad what was a bump up the backside on a coastal road hot enough to fry eggs on? Nothing.

By the time Kate throbbed the Mercedes up the pink gravel driveway it was gone six o'clock and her nerves were stretched. She was late for work, her cotton sundress was sticking to her with perspiration, her head was pounding and she was beginning to wonder if Conrad was all right. He'd rubbed his neck several times on the way home but had assured her he was fine, but now they'd stopped she noticed a cut and a rapidly developing bruise on his forehead where it had caught the mirror.

'Conrad!' Lorraine exclaimed shrilly, running over from the poolside, pulling a light towelling robe over her white swimsuit. 'Conrad, you're bleeding!'

Conrad, very pale, stood leaning against the side of the Mercedes and allowed Lorraine to inspect the cut, which looked far worse now he was in sunlight. Kate got out. Lorraine turned on her in fury.

'What have you done, Kate? Why are you driving and—?'

'What's this commotion?' Guy called out, coming across the terrace to join them.

Kate bit her lip, expecting the worst because it couldn't get any better. Already Lorraine was accusing her.

'We had an accident,' Kate admitted.

'Kate insisted on driving home and I shouldn't have let her,' Conrad put in. 'She isn't used to the traffic or the car.'

Kate drew in her breath. At the very least she had expected his support, not this suggestion that she was to blame. The accident hadn't been her fault and if he had been driving in his sorry state it could have been far worse.

Lorraine flung her a piercing look over the top of the Mercedes. '*You* were driving when you had the accident?' she screeched.

'Calm down, Lorraine,' Guy told her coldly. 'Take Conrad inside and tend to that wound.'

'She could have killed him,' Lorraine accused, throwing a last look of disdain at Kate. She took Conrad's arm and led him to the villa.

Kate watched them in abject misery. Suddenly Lorraine cared about Conrad. Suddenly the accident was her fault. Suddenly the world was too impossible to cope with.

'Are you all right, Kate?'

She swung round to Guy, honestly surprised that he was showing concern for her, but was it the calm before the storm? She'd disobeyed him and gone out and forgotten the mobile phone and couldn't fail to be in trouble.

'Perfectly all right,' she told him tartly, though she wasn't. It was all catching up on her and if she didn't get under a cool shower quick she was going to melt. 'I'm sorry about the damage to the car and your brother, but both will survive, no doubt,' she added sarcastically, and turned away from him.

Kate showered, trying to wash away her disgust with Conrad for not standing by her, and with Lorraine for her bitter accusations. Both experiences were doubly painful after what she'd put up with all afternoon—Conrad boring her ragged about his problems with the apparently recalcitrant Lorraine. Now Lorraine was all over him. She didn't understand any of them. They were all crazy.

Wrapping a huge towel around her and tucking the ends under her arms, she padded back to her bedroom, and took a sharp breath as she walked in.

Guy turned to her, his eyes dark and accusing. He had her glossy carrier bag in his hand and he up-ended it and the peacock silk creation slid out onto his other hand. He weighed it up and down and glared at her.

'You left this in the back of the car and Conrad told me where it came from. While you were dragging my brother and his credit cards around Puerto Banus I don't suppose for a minute you gave a thought to that vital call from Roederers? No, too busy satisfying your greed.' He flung the dress at her furiously and Kate instinctively caught it. 'Very pretty,' he drawled sarcastically. 'Was it worth it, Kate? Because it sure as hell cost the company plenty.'

She stared at him, shame biting at her for that lost phone call. Oh, why had she let Conrad talk her into going out with him? And now Guy thought her nothing but a silly shopaholic, dragging his brother around exclusive boutiques all afternoon. And what a creep Conrad was, losing no time in telling everyone how bountiful he had been. Another ploy to stir Lorraine's jealousy?

'All wide-eyed innocence again,' Guy went on contemptuously. 'My God, how you turn it on. You put Lorraine to shame.'

He shook his head, stepped towards her and lifted her damp chin. His eyes were as uncompromising as industrial steel. 'And there was I warning you about the games everyone plays and you are the grand master of them all. You're so determined to get your sticky little hands on my brother, you'll tread on everyone's feelings, to say nothing of losing the company money, to get him. After last night you knew the situation between Conrad and Lorraine but it didn't stop you having a last pitch at him.'

Kate swallowed, her eyes wide and plaintive. She jerked her chin free of his grasp. 'Stop it!' she cried. 'I...I didn't...I wasn't...' Her voice croaked to nothing. She was wasting her time. He wouldn't believe her. He would side with his brother every time. And Conrad was evil, so intent on using her to get at Lorraine that *he* had lost Latham's the deal, and then blamed her for the accident and made Guy believe he had bought her this dress. The injustice of it all swelled her strength again.

'What exactly bugs you the most, Guy—losing the German deal or the thought of me out sponging off your brother?'

'What do you think?' he accused bitterly.

She knew exactly—the deal—and it hurt so badly that she wanted to scream. She swallowed hard. 'I'm late,' she murmured fretfully. 'Will you please get out of my bedroom so I can dress?'

His eyes were murderous. 'You can't even deny that your intentions where my brother is concerned are as strong as ever.'

Her heart fluttered uncertainly. It sounded as if he was more concerned about her and Conrad than the Germans. But no, this was an added punishment, one aimed at her morals. Kate's eyes suddenly blazed with anger. She *had* denied it so what more did he want—blood?

'Why should I waste my breath and blood pressure? It's beneath me to deny it more than I already have. You can think what you like because it doesn't concern me,' she told him through thin lips.

'If you had any pride it should concern you, Kate,' he growled. 'After what you've done today I'd be quite within my rights to put you on the first flight back to the UK.'

Kate stiffened. She'd taken more than enough. 'But you won't, Guy,' she told him flintily. 'Your threats never take wing and more's the pity because nothing would give me greater pleasure than to be away from here. You put up with me because you have no choice but I don't have to put up with your accusations. Now I'll tell you something I should have told you from the off. My interest in Conrad from the start was minimal but now it's less than nothing. I wouldn't have your brother if he came gold-plated and hallmarked!'

His mouth twisted with distaste and his eyes narrowed to slits of contempt. 'Easy now to deny you want him when I have you cornered. You can't deny this evidence, though!' He disdainfully took a flick at the dress she clutched in her hands. 'Ill-gotten gains, Kate. I thought you above it.'

He went to turn away but Kate wouldn't let him. She slung the dress down, clutched at his arm and spun him back to face her. To think that she had wanted him by her side this afternoon, wanted his company, his spark, his arms around her. Her eyes flooded with tears and to cover herself she turned and snatched the carrier bag from the bed and plunged her hand in it to find the receipt.

She thrust it at him, hands trembling with anger. 'Look at that, Guy Latham. There won't be any card numbers you recognise as your brother's.' Her eyes searched the room for her bag. She darted to it and rummaged for her credit card and thrust it at him, eyes burning as if she had a fever.

'I paid for my own dress, Guy,' she croaked painfully. 'There, look. My credit-card number, my signature—'

'OK, OK,' he breathed, frowning down at the receipt and the card. 'Listen, I'm—'

'What? Sorry? Don't you dare apologise till I've finished,' she warned. 'Then you can apologise, for everything. I didn't want to go out with your brother this afternoon but...but he insisted, and do you know why he insisted? To make Lorraine jealous. He used me, just like you all do. Kate Stephens, the fall guy. If anything goes wrong, it's all my fault.'

'It's not like that—'

'It is!' Kate insisted, stepping back as he stepped forward as if to grasp hold of her. 'I can't even defend myself because you are brothers and loyal to each other, and it seems Lorraine belongs to the pair of you so I'm up against a brick wall there. Whatever I say, however I try to defend myself, it will never be right for you, or Conrad, or Lorraine!'

'I've told you, Lorraine means nothing to me and by now you should know she means everything to my brother.'

'After what I've been through this afternoon, don't I just!' Kate spiked sarcastically. 'I've had a hateful time today. As I said, I didn't want to go but Conrad insisted. I forgot the phone and then we went to this restaurant and...and...' Oh, it was hopeless. She couldn't tell tales even if she thought he would believe her. She sighed helplessly. 'Leave me alone, Guy,' she whispered. 'I've had enough of the lot of you today.'

He grasped her wrist and pulled it up in front of them both. Still angry with her, he bit out, 'Tell me everything that happened this afternoon.'

'No!' she stated flatly, her jawline set with determination.

His eyes blazed at her defiance. 'Tell me everything,' he ground out between his teeth. 'Or am I to believe the very worst?'

'No,' she protested vehemently. 'That isn't fair.'

'According to you, nothing is fair,' he grated maliciously. 'Poor little hard-done-by Kate. Innocent of all in her own estimation, a she-devil in everyone else's.'

'You bastard!' Kate cried, anger bursting the words from her lips. 'That is so damned unjust! Your brother embarrassed me beyond measure this afternoon, drinking too much, trying to buy me clothes. I had to drive home because he was incapable. The accident wasn't my fault; some idiot hit us from behind. I had to sort it all out because your damned brother was too drunk! I hated it all— listening to him going on and on about Lorraine, being with *him* when I wanted to be with you!'

With a gasp she bit her lower lip and coloured deeply. Her eyes flicked to his. She understood then what he had done—angered her enough to make her blurt out the truth. The whole truth . . . that she had wanted to be with him! And now she was, here in her bedroom, and wanting the ground to open under her.

Tenderly his hands came to her naked shoulders and his eyes softened. His body seemed to let go, as if relieved to shed the pent-up rage inside him.

'You don't know how long I've waited to hear you say that,' he breathed. He lowered his mouth to her feverish lips but she couldn't stand the pain of it. She shrank away from him in terror, knowing how close she was to total submission.

'Don't, Guy,' she pleaded, her voice just a plaintive whisper. 'I shouldn't have said what I did.'

'You meant it,' he said confidently.

Clutching the towel at her breasts, she shook her head, and damp hair fell across her cheek. He lifted a hand and his fingers brushed the wisps aside.

'You meant it, Kate,' he repeated, 'and I really don't understand why you fight it so. It's getting wearing for us both.'

'And if I stop fighting you will just accept that you have won and leave me alone?' she asked.

He smiled—a very small smile. 'It wouldn't be the end of it all, only the beginning. What are you afraid of?'

It was easy to tell him the truth now because she had given away so much about her feelings. 'I'm afraid of getting it all wrong,' she told him, with a dismissive shrug of her naked shoulders. 'Nothing more sinister than that. I came here admiring your brother and disliking you intensely. Now it seems I've done an about-turn. I don't think my judgement of men is worth very much, do you?'

'Frankly I don't think it matters,' he said softly.

No, it didn't, she realised with a sinking heart, not if insincerity was to the fore.

'It matters to me, Guy,' she said coldly. 'I've seen things here I couldn't have imagined and—'

'And it has attacked all your sensibilities because you live in a sterile world of your own making where sex is outlawed.'

Kate squared her shoulders. 'And sex is where it's all at,' she sneered.

'You know it, sweetheart,' he mocked. 'Trouble is, a lot of people deny it when a good old bout of honesty makes for an easier life. I'm honest with you so why can't you be honest with me?'

'Honesty isn't enough, Guy. Try sincerity for a change and you might get somewhere. You only want me because I'm a challenge to you. Suddenly you don't want Lorraine because she's a pushover. No doubt Conrad only wants Lorraine because she is crazy for you. Now Lorraine is going for Conrad because he has shown interest in me.'

She smirked at him. 'You know, the permutations are endless. I could stand here all night trotting them out to you, and they are all meaningless because every one of them is sadly lacking in sincerity and deep emotion and just about everything *I* want from a relationship.'

'So you want it all?'

'Yes, Guy,' she said stiffly. 'I want it all and I'm just a pleasurable pastime for you, something to spice up our time here, one of your games to while away the non-working, non-profit-making hours.'

His eyes darkened in anger and Kate knew she had hit the truth, otherwise he would have simply smiled at her indulgently.

'Never that, Kate. You have some quirky preconceived ideas of what goes on in a man's head, all of them way off the mark. You talk of honesty; try this.' He caught the outside seam of her towel and tugged at it. In panic Kate grasped it but the ends had come undone and they swung down, scarcely covering her breasts as she clutched the rest to her chin. 'There, now you have my honesty, my need for you. I want to make love to you. I've fought it and can't fight it any more. I've been patient and now I'm not any more. Is that honest enough for you?'

She couldn't answer. Her throat was too dry, her quickening heartbeat too irregular. Her skin burned as if he were already caressing it.

'Well, answer me,' he ordered roughly. 'Give me some indication that my honesty is enough for you.'

She nodded.

'Good. Now you want my sincerity.' He tugged the towel so hard this time that it jerked from her fingers and she was naked in front of him. An overpowering heat invaded her flesh at the unexpected exposure, the sensation making her sway dizzily. He ran the backs of his fingers down the front of her, trailing a white-hot trail of pure desire down between her breasts, over her waist to the smooth flatness of her stomach. A touch so light and fearless and caring that her eyes widened expectantly.

'The touch of sincerity you crave,' he whispered. 'The touch that tells you you are wrong to think so badly of me.'

This time when his lips came to hers she was unable to draw back. The sweet tenderness that his touch promised overwhelmed her with need. Somewhere in the back of her consciousness a weak warning pulsed, so very vague now that he was kissing her so deeply and holding her naked body so firmly against him. She believed in his honesty and wanted to believe in his sincerity, but it wasn't easy. Then suddenly it was very easy as he drew back from her and looked deep into her eyes. She saw a depth of emotion and desire that she knew wasn't contrived.

'Now, Kate,' he murmured softly, cupping her face in both hands and holding her tenderly. 'I want you now.'

Her heart was possessed as she gazed up at him, in his control and no one else's. She couldn't argue or draw away from him because she was his and wanted to be his. He saw the acceptance in her misty eyes and smiled his acknowledgement, and it was all that was needed.

Effortlessly he lifted her, laid her on the bed and leaned down over her, smoothing small kisses over her brow as he loosened the belt at his trousers. Then he was easing down beside her and she clung to him, burying her face in his neck, aching with need for him.

In the hazy distance the mobile phone trilled and Kate's heart stopped. How cruel and how ironic. She tried to tell him, parted her moist lips, but he stilled them with his own, hot and passionate and unrelenting.

'This is more important,' he breathed roughly against her throat, and to Kate they were the most wonderful words she had every heard.

CHAPTER EIGHT

THEIR naked flesh merged in a fury of need, blocking out all life apart from each other. Their mouths were as one, deeply penetrating in their exploration, their caresses all sensual discovery. Kate's body blossomed under such skilled expertise and she gave herself to him completely—every inch, every pulse, every breath.

His body was glistening, magnificent, pressed against her side as his exploration of her deepened. The fierce arousal it evoked in her took her breath away. He was hard and powerful, aroused and taut, and she was almost frightened of the need he would surely demand from her.

He moved restlessly now, breathing hard, his mouth so passionate against her throat, her breasts. She cried out and trembled against him as he drew on her aching nipples. The sensation was beyond her experience, a new, fierce sensation of sensuality and desire. She was moist and yielding and demanding. She lost all thought but one of heady pleasure, wanting her own and anxious to give it.

Her hands clawed down his back to his hips, which were moving rhythmically against hers in a parody of lovemaking, rubbing backwards and forwards. She touched him and thrilled to his shuddering intake of breath as she wantonly smoothed her fingers around him.

He ran a hand across her thigh and between her legs. Without thinking she arched herself against his penetrating caresses, her head reeling with the sweet, sweet pressure that fired her so deeply. Heat engulfed her and the sensation of losing control was hurling her into another world.

Kate lost it all, all reasoning, as he positioned himself over her and then pressed into her so completely and passionately that it was as if they were programmed solely for each other. Deep, deep into her hot, suppliant body, sending her into a paroxysm of animal desire, till she moved as vibrantly as he, riding with him, unified in passionate intent, closer, closer.

Kate burned and swelled and cried out, and Guy held her hips and moved so erotically inside her that her climax knew no control. It burst inside her, hot, fluid, washing through her body in wave after wave of pulsing pressure.

Guy let out a primeval cry of triumph and shuddered against her in one final thrust of urgency, and then collapsed over her, his breath long and drawn out, his body burning against hers.

Kate's eyes ached as if she had a fever as she lay under him, tenderly drawing her fingers through his damp hair, trying to regulate her own ragged breathing while listening to his levelling. He moved off her but cradled her in one arm and grazed the other down her body, retracing the soft, tender caresses that had aroused her so passionately.

Slowly reality seeped into her—an unwelcome reality that she didn't want to face. She loved him and she hadn't wanted to fall in love and it was why she had never admitted her attraction to him from the start. It was almost a paranoia, a fear of being used and hurt as she had been by Gustav and as her mother had been by her father. She bit her lip and turned her face to look at him lying next to her, eyes closed, breath even now.

He had said he had fought her. He hadn't wanted this to happen and she believed him. She had refused to acknowledge him, her fear building a barrier against him till she had convinced herself that he was the most loathsome man that had ever drawn breath. But what were his reasons for holding back from her so long—a similar fear of rejection?

'Try and think of something original to say,' he murmured without opening his eyes. 'I couldn't bear it if you said you were sorry it happened.'

Kate smiled and whispered, '"My Lord, I shall reply amazedly, Half sleep, half waking. But as yet, I swear, I cannot truly say how I came here..."'

He rose up onto one elbow to look down on her in astonishment.

'Shakespeare,' she told him with a smile. 'I played Lysander in a school production of *A Midsummer Night's Dream*.'

'You obviously had a gender problem then that you haven't now,' he teased, running a hand across her breast.

'All-girls' school. The tallest had to take men's roles. Was it original enough for you?'

'Unique.' He smiled and bent to kiss her nose.

'Guy,' she murmured, serious now, 'I truly don't know how I came to be here.'

'It was inevitable, Kate. Two forces hitting head-on. Inevitable and unavoidable.'

And inconsequential? she wondered, but dared not ask. The thought sobered her, though.

'And now so serious,' he murmured. 'Don't even think about it, Kate.' The pressure on her breast increased and as he rushed a kiss across her warm lips her arousal was as swift as his.

In the heat of a fading Mediterranean day they turned to each other and lost themselves in a secret world of tender touches, heated kisses and perfumed secrets...

Charo told them later—bursting into the courtyard where Kate and Guy drank wine by candlelight and talked softly under the vines. An ambulance was on its way for Conrad Latham.

Kate and Guy shot to their feet. 'What happened, Charo?' Guy asked.

Charo stood wringing her hands. 'He say he have pain in his arm and his chest and—'

'God, his heart!' Guy grated, and flew from the courtyard. Kate went to follow but Charo stopped her.

'It's all right, *señorita*. Too many people is not good.'

'Oh, Charo,' Kate moaned, wrapping her arms around herself, feeling sick inside. 'The...the accident this afternoon...it must have brought on...' She couldn't finish; the implications that it was her fault were too terrible for words.

'No, it is not your fault,' Charo insisted, but Kate heard her words as if in an echo chamber, over and over again. It *was* her fault otherwise Charo wouldn't be reassuring her that it *wasn't*.

She had a long night ahead of her in which to reflect on it all after Charo left. If only she had refused point-blank to go out with Conrad this would never have happened. He had drunk too much, the accident had shaken him, and the stress of it all had brought on a heart attack.

Kate sat alone in the hot courtyard, sipping wine to deaden the thought that when it had happened she and Guy had been making love . . . She blocked it out—everything. She couldn't even bear to think of what had happened between her and Guy. She wanted to sleep and wake up and find that it had all been a nightmare.

She didn't sleep. She lay in the bed she and Guy had made love in and Guy didn't come back, and she thought the very worst—that Conrad had died and it was her fault.

'Thank God,' Kate breathed at breakfast in the courtyard the next morning.

Charo grinned as she poured Kate's coffee. 'He will be able to come home later this afternoon, after they fit a special collar. Señor Latham, he won't like that.'

'It's better than a heart attack,' Kate ruefully commented.

She was enormously relieved that Conrad had only suffered a small broken bone in his neck—a whiplash injury that sounded far more extreme than it was. And if he had worn his seat belt it might not have happened. Kate felt unburdened of her guilt but doubted anyone else would absolve her so easily.

'I'd better get ready for work, then,' Kate said, getting up from the breakfast table. She hadn't dressed yet, had just slipped on her robe when she'd heard Charo moving about in the kitchen below. Actually she hadn't known it was Charo and had expected to see Guy, tired and dishevelled after a night at the hospital. She had flown down the stone stairs, expecting the worst, and been surprised to find Charo preparing her breakfast, cheerily ready to impart the good news that Conrad was well and coming home.

'*Sí*, Señor Latham, he work already,' Charo told her as she turned into the house with the breakfast things.

Kate followed, her insides crawling. 'You mean Guy?' she husked from the kitchen archway. 'He's back from the hospital?'

'*Sí*. He was back last night. He stay at the villa, with Señorita Lorraine.'

A deep chill went down Kate's spine and her legs were leaden as she went upstairs. Closing her bedroom door after her, she leaned back on it before her legs gave way altogether. Guy and Lorraine, together in the villa while Conrad spent the night in the hospital. Guy hadn't come back to the guest house and Kate had presumed he'd been at the hospital with his brother all night.

Oh, God, she might have known; she *should* have known. None of them could be trusted—no man and especially not Guy. She'd known what he was like yet she had weakened and allowed him her heart and really that was all he had wanted—her total submission. Game over and won.

Kate walked across the room and stood at the open window, trembling in spite of the heat. The cicadas still buzzed, the jasmine was still sweet and heady on the air; life went on as if nothing had happened. But everything had happened. She was in love with a man who could never change—a deceiver of hearts, a man who had used her and discarded her.

She dressed slowly, dreading facing him, wishing she had Lorraine's experience . . . Lorraine—what sort of a woman was she to toss her affections around so lightly? Guy, Conrad, Guy again. *Guy again*. The thought tore at her very being. How could he have stayed with Lorraine after their evening of passion?

'Kate, sweetheart, I can't stop,' Guy told her as she stepped into the office. 'With Conrad out of action I'm up to my eyes in it and later I have to pick him up from the hospital.' He seemed to have an obsession with shuffling papers; he was always at it, Kate thought inconsequentially. 'Charo's told you everything, of course.' He stopped shuffling and looked across at her. He looked drained and so he should, she supposed, trying not to think.

'Yes, of course,' Kate said tightly. 'Getting my information from the maid again.'

She saw his shoulders stiffen. 'It's been a hell of a night, Kate, and I don't need—'

'I'm sorry,' Kate said quickly, but she wasn't. She turned to her desk and suddenly felt him behind her and she spun around. He gripped her shoulders before she could move out of range. She couldn't even read his eyes this morning, they were so impenetrable.

'Don't give me a hard time, Kate. That apology came without feeling and I know exactly what is going through your mind. No one blames you for what happened to Conrad.'

Nothing had been further from her thoughts! Conrad had only himself to blame for his injury. She had warned him about his seat belt and the accident hadn't been her fault, and she had dealt with it all in her own head once she'd known Conrad's problem wasn't terminal. But Guy's problems were terminal. If he didn't know what was bothering her this morning, what hope was there for him?

Kate steeled herself under his touch, which she supposed he thought was reassuring. 'Why mention it, then, if it isn't foremost in your mind?'

'It isn't, Kate.'

'It is, Guy,' she insisted. 'It was practically the first thing you said to me just now. Charo said the same thing: it wasn't my fault. What escapes you all is that I *know* it wasn't my fault and that isn't what is bugging me this morning.'

He still held her firmly by her shoulders. 'So what is?'

Her voice rose. 'You don't know?'

'I wouldn't ask if I did,' he snapped, and then his eyes darkened with realisation. 'Don't play that woman's game with me, Kate. Don't tell me you're questioning what happened between us—'

Furiously she shook herself out of his clutches, her eyes blazing with the shock of his insensitivity.

'The whys and wherefores of sex were the last things on my mind last night, Guy Latham. You take me for some silly, frivolous female with nothing but romance and moonlight and roses misting my thoughts. Wrong. I've had one hell of a night too, worrying myself sick about Conrad—'

His eyes fired and he grasped her shoulders again. His voice was thick. 'Worried sick about Conrad? After we've made love you still have an unhealthy interest in my brother?'

'You idiot, Guy,' Kate blazed. 'And stop grabbing at my shoulders every minute! I'm not about to run away till I've had my say.'

She shook herself free once again. 'Yes, I was worried about your brother; it's called concern—something you might be wise to remember in the future. You afforded me none last night. You left here believing he'd had a heart attack and till this morning I didn't know he hadn't! I was worried all night because I thought the accident had precipitated it and I had been with him at the time. I *know* it wasn't my fault but you can't avoid the thought that if only...'

She raised her chin defiantly, looked him straight in the eye and her tone took on a new accusing sharpness. 'Thanks, Guy, for putting my mind at rest last night. At the very least you might have popped in to tell me Conrad was OK before *comforting* Lorraine at the villa.'

His whole body stiffened and then seemed to sag in one movement. His eyes never left hers.

'Kate, darling,' he said roughly, 'it was a bad night. I was worried about Conrad and—'

'And Lorraine needed comforting and I was the last person in your thoughts.' She held her palms up to him as if to ward him off but he hadn't moved. 'It doesn't matter, Guy; it just con-firms—'

'Don't, Kate,' he suddenly warned. 'I'm not in-fallible. I'm not Superman. Last night I got it all wrong.'

She stung inside. He had admitted it and she hadn't expected that he would be so cruelly open about it. The pain caused her to defend herself the only way she could—by telling him the very same.

'And so did I, Guy. I got it very wrong, all of it, so let's put it down to experience and forget it. As far as I am concerned what happened between us last evening was a non-event.' She held his eyes with hers, oh, so steadily, oh, so unemotionally. It hurt to do it but there was no other way out. He must never know how deeply she cared for him.

His lips thinned as he spoke slowly and gravely. 'I didn't mean I got it wrong with you and me, Kate. I meant that I made a mistake in not waking you last night to tell you Conrad was safe. I came straight over to the guest house but there were no lights on and I didn't want to disturb you.' His eyes narrowed and his voice growled threateningly as he went on. 'I'm glad I didn't now because otherwise I might never have known just how fickle you are. A non-event, eh?' He shook his head. 'My God, what a fool I've been.'

He turned away, eyes hard and ungiving, shoulders stiff with tension, and strode out of the room. Kate clenched her fists at her sides, her nails digging into her palms. And what a fool she had been too. She should have waited to listen to his explanation for last night, because it was under-standable—he'd seen no lights burning... But what

wasn't understandable was his staying the night with
Lorraine at the villa. No, she wasn't a fool, she
decided fiercely, but he obviously took her for one.

Eventually she moved and sat down at her computer, and after half an hour knew it was useless.
Her head was thick and muzzy. She couldn't concentrate, and as she raked a hand through her hair
she knew what she had to do.

'You have to be joking!' Guy roared when Kate
told him her intention on his return to the guest
house late in the afternoon.

From the gardens at the side of the villa she'd
watched him and Lorraine return with a subdued
Conrad sporting a huge surgical collar that did
nothing for his image. While they'd been getting
out of the Mercedes, Kate had sped back to the
guest house to wait for Guy at the table in the
courtyard.

'You can't stop me, Guy,' she told him strongly.
'My formal resignation is on your desk and I'm
going back to the UK, tonight.'

Guy gave her a black look and poured himself a
glass of wine. Kate had opened it while waiting and
drunk a glass, and it had steadied her nerves and
given her strength to face him. She could easily have
left without seeing him, but facing him would act
as some sort of exorcism. He'd be mad with her
for walking out and would say hurtful things to
her, and she wanted to hear them because it would
reaffirm what a mistake she had made in falling in
love with him.

'You are going nowhere tonight, Kate,' he told
her, deadly earnest, defying her to question him,

'other than to the villa for dinner—a welcome-home party for Conrad.'

Kate spluttered out a contemptuous laugh and looked up at him standing by the table. 'Dine with the wolves? No, thanks. I'm choosy who I dine with. Málaga airport cafeteria has come to hold a distinct charm since I've been forced to dine with the Lathams.'

He looked at her over the rim of his glass. 'You are not going, Kate. I do not accept your resignation and I sincerely hope you haven't wasted your time packing—'

'It was a pleasure to do it,' she taunted.

'It will be a penance to undo it, then. And just one small point before you try to defy me yet again. It's the height of the season and the chances of you getting a flight back to the UK tonight are about even to winning the state lottery without the purchase of a ticket.'

Kate raised her chin triumphantly. 'I phoned the airport and because of the rescheduling of certain flights some passengers have been rerouted to Heathrow. Someone else's misfortune is my gain. If I get to the airport in time I'm on this evening's flight.'

He gave her a cynical smile to accompany the black anger in his eyes. 'Very fortunate for you but useless. I won't allow it. We dine at the usual time tonight. Be there.' He put down his glass and went to go into the house.

'No, Guy,' Kate said firmly. She stood up to add weight to her determination. He turned from the door, eyes dark and narrowed in anger that she could be so defiant. 'I am going. I don't have a job

here any more. I don't want to be here and I won't
be. It's all spoilt. You've spoilt it all. I absolutely
refuse to stay.'

To her astonishment he smiled at her. 'Suit
yourself, then, Kate. You win, I lose. It wasn't much
of a battle, was it? Hardly worth it—a non-event,
as you said. I wish you well for your future.' He
went into the house without a backward glance at
her, his parting words hanging in the air with no
conviction or sincerity.

Kate stared at the doorway he'd disappeared
through, her mouth opening and shutting silently.
He'd given up, just like that; scarcely a fight, one
feeble   attempt   to   bring   her   down   and
then...nothing. She slumped back down to her seat
and poured herself some more wine but didn't drink
it. She glared at it crossly, knowing it had clouded
her thinking. She had wanted him to exert his authority and insist she stay, and wasn't that just a silly
female way to act? Contrary at the very least.

She fed the wine to the nearest potted plant, a
green succulent similar in stature to the aloe that
Guy had soothed her burning thigh with. The tears
came then, hot and thick and blinding her with
pain. She swept them away with the back of her
hand before he came down and found her crying
and thought that she cared. But it was useless, like
trying to stop a dam overflowing with a sponge.

Shakily she got up, went through the arched
doorway into the gardens, and wandered aimlessly,
not seeing anything and trying not to think how
miserably she had failed herself. Love wasn't for
her. It never worked out because she always fell for
the wrong men. Correction. She'd fallen for *one*

wrong man—Guy Latham; Gustav had been milk and water, whereas Guy was the *crème de la crème*. She had tried to fight him, she supposed, but he had overwhelmed her in the end, just as he had intended.

It was as hot as ever as she lingered on the scented path he had walked along with her that first time, the time he had accused her of throwing herself at him during one of her dizzy flights of fantasy. To this day she still didn't know if she had. But it didn't matter any more. Nothing mattered.

She stepped back into the courtyard and took one last look around. She had loved this place, loved his taste in furnishing it so simply. And she had loved him here. Biting back a fresh flood of tears and steeling herself inwardly, she went inside the house and looked around for the mobile phone. She'd already taken a note of the number of a Marbella taxi company after she had written her resignation in the office. She was going and her silly emotions were not going to stop her.

'You rat, Guy Latham,' she muttered under her breath, searching in vain for the mobile. 'Guy!' she shouted up the stairs, and leapt up them two at a time. He wasn't going to get away with this. She needed a taxi to get out of here because for sure he wouldn't drive her to the airport.

He'd gone. Kate stood in the doorway of her bedroom and gulped fiercely, hardly able to believe what she couldn't see—her suitcase and airline bag. She'd left them packed and ready at the foot of the bed. She snatched at her handbag on the dressing table. Thank goodness he hadn't taken her money and passport. Faint with rage, Kate slumped onto the edge of the bed and leaned her head in her hands. He didn't want her to go—that was glaringly obvious—but for what reason?

Her heart began to pulse feebly. He needed her in a business sense but could it be more? He had taken her bags to stop her going but if she was so determined and hated him she'd go without the bags. So he was giving her a choice, giving her the opportunity to retract her decisions if she wanted to, or flee with her passport if she was so determined.

'Oh, I don't want to go,' she breathed miserably into the balmy night air. He had stayed with Lorraine last night but that didn't mean to say... She bit her lip and stared down at the peacock-blue silk dress that lay on the bed next to her. She'd left it out of her packing because it was a painful reminder—of Guy believing Conrad had bought it, of Conrad leading everyone to believe he had.

Kate stood up and held it to her in front of the full-length mirror on the wall. Her heart squeezed. He could have taken this too but he had left it in the hope that she would wear it to dinner tonight. She couldn't go dressed in the cotton trousers and T-shirt she was wearing for travelling in.

It was a very beautiful dress and perhaps Guy would realise... She crumpled it and tossed it down on the bed. If he didn't love her after their night of passion he never would, and a wretched dress wouldn't make any difference.

They were seating themselves at the long table on the terrace of the villa when Kate got there. Guy saw her first and, with a totally unsurprised expression on his face, came to the terrace steps to greet her.

Kate's pulses raced as he took her elbow and leaned close to her ear to whisper, 'So you changed your mind. I knew you would.'

'You left me no choice,' she returned.

Guy made no comment but then she supposed he wouldn't now that he was pulling her chair out for her and everyone was watching them.

Kate sat down and smiled tentatively at Lorraine, who offered no such courtesy in return, only an accusing glare. Conrad at least afforded her a pleasant welcoming smile, in spite of the fact that his face looked drawn. To his credit he had made an effort, as he and Guy always did for the evening meal, and he looked coolly elegant in a lightweight evening suit despite the clumsy-looking collar at his neck.

'I'm sorry about your neck, Conrad,' Kate began sincerely. 'I hope—'

'And so you should be,' Lorraine cut in spitefully. 'It could have been so much worse for Conrad—'

'But it wasn't, Lorraine,' Guy interjected calmly. 'Let's leave it alone, shall we?'

'No, we won't,' Lorraine insisted, defying him.

Kate bit her lower lip, amazed at Lorraine's biting thrusts. She usually simpered in Guy's company.

'It's not to be tossed aside so casually,' Lorraine went on. 'Kate did a foolish thing and Conrad suffered and—'

'I said that's *enough*,' Guy emphasised, so heatedly this time that even the cicadas seemed to fall silent. 'Let's eat.'

Kate stared down at the smoked salmon in front of her while Guy popped a champagne cork to welcome Conrad home—anyone would have thought he'd returned after major heart surgery, she thought grimly. She felt sick to the very marrow. Why didn't Conrad speak up for her? Though debilitated by drink he hadn't been so drunk that he hadn't known what had happened. Kate regretted her decision to join them for dinner. She should have left as planned and not allowed her romantic notion that Guy cared for her to sway her.

The conversation turned to the drop in interest rates in the UK as they ate, but there was such an underlying throb of tension in the air that Kate wondered if there was something going on that she didn't know about. As they talked she observed them, and thought that not a lot had changed since they had all started working together.

Tension. Every meal with them was loaded with tension. Guy and Conrad might be brothers and partners but they didn't appear to be close. And Lorraine was...ever Lorraine, scowling at everyone, even Guy now. Poor Lorraine, she must be a pretty unhappy lady in spite of having two very eligible bachelors at her beck and call, Kate mused.

Charo served the next course, and, probably because of an animated conversation going on between Guy and Conrad at opposite ends of the table, she leaned towards her and whispered, 'I sorry about your bags, *señorita*.'

'My bags?' Kate frowned.

'*Sí*. I move them into the wardrobe and one fall open and everything fall out. I have no time to do it properly. Tomorrow I do it.' She moved away and Kate sat bleakly staring at her plate again.

Guy hadn't taken them to force her into a decision. Charo had put them in the wardrobe. And Kate, love-struck and dozy, hadn't even checked the wretched wardrobe. And if she had she wouldn't be sitting here and suffering so miserably. Guy Latham didn't want her. He had given her no choice because she didn't matter to him.

'So you do have another dress, Kate.' Lorraine's voice broke into her misery. 'And very pretty it is too.'

'Isn't that the dress I bought you in Puerto Banus?' Conrad enquired. 'I always have prided myself on my taste—'

'No, it is not the dress you bought me in Puerto Banus!' Kate suddenly cried, leaping to her feet in fury. She'd had enough—more than enough. She didn't have to suffer this and she wouldn't. 'It's the dress I bought *myself*, Conrad. You *thought* you had bought it because—'

'That's enough, Kate,' Guy said, as if talking to an emotional child ready to throw a tantrum. He got to his feet as if intending to come around the table to her.

Kate stood her ground and glared furiously at each of them in turn.

'I will not shut up, Guy. I refuse to take any more from the lot of you. You didn't buy this dress, Conrad. You were too drunk to realise what was going on—'

Lorraine let out a sob of protest and Kate turned on her. 'Yes, drunk, Lorraine. Too drunk to drive, and that is why I drove the car back. The accident wasn't my fault. You can't back a stationary car into the front of a moving vegetable lorry! Conrad is wearing that collar now because he was too drunk to wear his seat belt. Conrad knows all this but for some unaccountable reason won't admit it.'

She threw her napkin down on the polished surface of the table. 'Please excuse me. I have no wish to continue this meal and be accused and denigrated and sneered at. Goodnight.'

In silence, Kate moved away from the table. Guy slumped down into his seat, rubbing his forehead. Conrad coloured hotly above his collar and tried to ease it away from his neck. Lorraine stared at Kate as if she had gone insane. No one stopped her as she walked through the gardens to the old guest house. But then she hadn't expected anyone to.

CHAPTER NINE

KATE was about to haul her bags down the stairs the next morning when Guy came out of his bedroom. He'd returned to the guest house in the early hours of the morning. She'd been lying stiff and anguished in bed and had heard his bedroom door close after him and she'd thought in that moment of dismay that that was the very worst thing of all about the evening. He might at the very least have tried to talk to her.

'Not another feeble attempt to leave,' he murmured. He was dressed for work and it was another put-down for Kate. To him, life went on, regardless.

She let go of the bags and faced him. 'Not feeble this time, determined.'

'Kate, we need to talk.'

'What about? Your brother's surgical collar that's my fault, the silk dress the world thinks your brother bought for me? And what about—'

'What about coffee?' he suggested, and brushed past her to the stairs. 'Leave those bags.'

Charo was in the kitchen making the breakfast so neither spoke but to make small talk. It was very hot under the shades and the scent from the jasmine was almost overpowering this morning. Kate sat at the table and waited for Charo to pour her coffee and felt so miserable that she couldn't even summon a smile for her.

'I don't want you to leave, Kate,' Guy told her when Charo had left them with the coffee-pot, fresh rolls and jam.

'I'm sure you don't,' she agreed. 'But Lorraine is quite capable—'

'To hell with Lorraine. It's you I want, not Lorraine,' he growled.

Yes, he needed her business skills and little else, and as for not wanting Lorraine…he'd wanted her enough on the night Conrad had gone to hospital.

'But I don't want any of you. Last night was the last straw.' Kate looked at him intently. 'Guy, I'm not sorry for my outburst last night. It needed to be said and for sure you weren't going to speak up for me, were you?'

He met her gaze with equal intensity. 'I didn't think it necessary to speak up for you when you are quite capable of doing all right for yourself. My brother overreacts at times but he isn't the ogre you think. He winds himself up over Lorraine sometimes and acts the way he does out of defence of his emotions. I did warn you about him, Kate.'

'Yes, you did and I know Lorraine for myself, but I honestly didn't expect all this—all of you playing these weird emotional games, with me as the common denominator. All of you have used me, abused me and hurt me.'

'You think that of me?' he asked gravely.

'Especially you,' she murmured, toying with her coffee-spoon.

He leaned across the table to her and took her hand. 'Not me, Kate. I have never used you and have never had any intention to hurt you—'

'But you do hurt me, all the time. I never wanted to...' She'd been about to say fall in love with him but stopped just in time. That would have been the last humiliation. She pulled her hand out from under his, hating herself for letting the small tender touch get to her heart. 'We...we shouldn't have made love, Guy,' she went on in a haunting whisper. 'It changes everything. I *have* to leave the company now because it is all too embarrassing to stay.'

'Our lovemaking was embarrassing, was it?'

She shook her head. 'No...no, of course not, but the situation is embarrassing.'

'I don't understand,' he sighed.

Kate looked at him long and hard as he poured coffee. No, being Guy 'Lothario' Latham, he wouldn't understand. How could she face him in the London office, knowing him so intimately, having made love to him? The girls would gossip as usual and who knew how many of them he had...?

She stood up quickly, the thought of him and other women dragging at her insides. This was all about trust and she didn't trust him, and besides, what were his intentions? To carry on this affair, or was she just a passing challenge to him? She'd never know because she wouldn't ask and he wasn't the sort to volunteer any such information.

'Where are you going?'

She couldn't answer because she was all choked up inside, her throat raw at the thought that she had been so weak and allowed love into her heart when she hadn't the wherewithal to cope with it.

He caught her up in her bedroom and swung her around to face him.

'You are not leaving—at least not till we have sorted this out,' he grated angrily. 'Everything would have been OK if Conrad hadn't gone to the hospital. We were all right that night. We made love, we sat in the courtyard talking—'

'And then you left,' Kate bit out spitefully, 'and you didn't come back. You stayed with Lorraine all night—'

'Under the same roof,' he interrupted fiercely.

'Yes, like us under the same roof, and look what happened!'

His eyes blazed and his grip on her bit painfully into her upper arm. 'One bad experience in your life and you think all men are tainted the same way. You have no trust in you—'

'You don't offer it, Guy. Everyone knows you and Lorraine—'

'Office gossip, or has she led you to believe there is more to our association?' He sneered.

'I don't have to be led to believe. I've seen it: clinches in the office, shopping trips every afternoon, smoochy dancing—oh, a million other give-away signs that scream out that you—'

'And Lorraine are having an affair,' he finished for her.

Her stomach tightened. 'You admit it, then?'

'I shouldn't have to,' he ground out angrily. 'You should know that I couldn't have made love to you the way I did if I was having an affair with another woman. You've put your own interpretation on everything you have seen of Lorraine and me. Clinches in the office: did you see my arms around her? Did you see our mouths actually touching?'

'No, but—'

'And those supposed shopping trips were business meetings, as I told you—'

'Yes, but—'

'And smoochy dancing. Who asked who to dance?'

'But—'

'No more buts, Kate. You won't believe it because you don't want to. It's so much easier to cop out of a relationship, using your bruised little ego as leverage. What is it with you? Aren't you capable of a normal relationship?'

She shook herself free of him then, skin pale and damp, pulses throbbing with the awful realisation that he was probably right. She hadn't a chance with the poison still inside her. After her mother's failed marriage and her own bitter experience with Gustav, what hope had she?

'A "normal relationship" with you, I suppose, would be me waiting for you to come in with the milk. Watching you flirting outrageously and Lorraine—'

'Lorraine is nothing in my life!'

'I can't believe you!' she screamed back at him.

His eyes were hard and unyielding and when he spoke his words were harshly determined. 'I'm not fighting for you, Kate. I'm not fighting mistrust because it's not my fight to have; it's yours. You will make the decision about where we go from here because you are the one finding it difficult to cope with.'

He turned and left her standing in the middle of her bedroom, hot and trembling now, knowing it was all hopeless because that was his cop-out, making her take the choice, throwing the guilt onto her shoulders.

She sat on the edge of the bed and stared at the floor, stiff with tension, raw with pain inside. He didn't care very much for her at all. If he did he would tell her what she wanted to hear instead of forcing decisions on her—decisions she couldn't make. She wanted to trust him but couldn't because it wasn't enough that he denied an affair with Lorraine.

Lorraine had always led her to believe there was something between them . . . but, there again, to an outsider it would appear that it was Lorraine and Conrad now. Kate let out a mournful sigh. She didn't understand life or any of them.

'*Señorita.*' Charo poked her head around the edge of the door. 'Señorita Lorraine . . . she won't come in. She want you in the courtyard.'

Another warning, another 'keep off' threat! Kate got to her feet. Well, Lorraine Hunter had caught her at just the right time. Last night should have been a warning to her that she wasn't taking any more from any of them.

'What is it now?' Kate grated at Lorraine, who sat at the courtyard table helping herself to what was left of the breakfast coffee.

She turned as Kate spoke and Kate drew in her breath at the sight of Lorraine's face. She looked so pale and drawn—even vulnerable, if vulnerable could ever be applicable to the glossy red-gold blonde.

'What's wrong?' Kate breathed. 'Conrad—is he all right?'

Lorraine made a vague attempt at a smile, gazed down at her coffee and shook her head. 'Fine in the way you mean, not so fine otherwise. He and Guy are kicking up a storm with each other this morning'

Before asking why, Kate asked Charo, who was hovering in the doorway, to bring fresh coffee. She sat down across from Lorraine, thinking that if Guy and Conrad were rowing it would somehow be her fault.

'I came to apologise, Kate,' Lorraine started before Kate could speak. 'I've been unfair to you. After your outburst last night Conrad admitted he'd had a few too many that day you went out together. Apparently I had been giving him a hard time and he wasn't coping, and he admitted he'd behaved badly to you. He's very remorseful now. Then Guy told us about the dress.' She lifted her face to give Kate a small smile. 'Poor Conrad, he must have been in a state that day; he honestly thought he'd bought you that dress.'

Kate's acknowledging smile was more a grimace of the bad memory. Charo brought the coffee and fresh cups and then excused herself to go over to help in the villa. Kate poured the coffee, waiting for Lorraine to carry on because she really had nothing to offer herself.

'I've always been jealous of you, Kate,' Lorraine admitted as she stirred her coffee thoughtfully. 'I can tell you that now because you've won.'

'Won?' Kate breathed faintly, shocked by Lorraine's admission.

Some of the old Lorraine surfaced as she gave a small smirk and said thinly, 'You can stop that

innocent act now. Your ploy worked; you have him.
Kate Stephens did what no other woman has done
before: snared Guy Latham.'

Kate flushed deeply. Where had Lorraine got that
idea from? She might have had an evening of
passion with Guy but she certainly hadn't captured
him as Lorraine was suggesting. If anyone had a
claim to Guy's heart it was surely Lorraine.

'I suppose I knew from the day you joined the
company that you were trouble. Perhaps if I had
taken notice of your technique I might have got
Guy for myself. I just didn't think him the sort to
fall for an old trick like that. He obviously couldn't
resist the challenge and the chase.'

And got what he wanted and then . . . nothing,
Kate thought miserably.

'I needed Guy, you see. I wanted him to give me
back my pride after the way Conrad treated me last
year.' She looked at Kate and smiled hesitantly at
the astonished look on her face. She went on,
'Conrad and I had an affair and . . . and, well, it
didn't work out. We quarrelled and . . .'

She shrugged and her bottom lip trembled and
Kate could hardly believe what she was hearing.
'No one ever knew. It wasn't something I could
talk about. Conrad really hurt me and I had to work
at it to get him out of my system. I convinced myself
I hated him. Guy was always supportive and I
suppose I got hold of the wrong end of the stick,
took his kindness for something else.' She shrugged
again and gazed at Kate, almost willing her to
understand.

Stupefied, Kate stared at her. Was she hearing right? She tried to move her lips to form words but her mouth was so dry. She made it at last.

'Lorraine,' she croaked. 'You and Conrad—'

'He wants me back and I want to be back with him,' Lorraine said. She leaned closer to Kate across the table. Girl talk. A month ago Kate would have recoiled from gossip but now she suddenly wanted to know it all.

'I find it all terribly confusing,' she went on, with a shrug of her slightly padded shoulders. 'As I said, I was jealous of you because I saw the way Guy looked at you. You were so cool with him and he just played it cool. Then when we got here and I found he'd put you in this place with him, well, I thought all was lost.

'Then Conrad started playing his games, using you as bait. It worked. I was even more jealous of you. And then it hit me. I was more jealous of you with Conrad than of you with Guy. So why was I so jealous when I'd convinced myself I hated Conrad?' She looked startled suddenly. 'What have I said that's so funny?'

Kate waved a hand at her, trying to suppress the laughter. Lorraine was gabbling on so fast, it was hard to keep up with her, but what really amused Kate was that Lorraine's situation was so similar to her own. They had both convinced themselves that they hated the men they really loved. 'I'll tell you in a minute. Go on; I want to know about you and Conrad.'

Lorraine gave her a quizzical look. 'You know, you are a mystery, Kate. You never gossip at work and now you are lapping it up. Anyway, to get back to me and Conrad . . . well, I knew for sure I loved him when you came back after that accident. He looked so crumpled and unhappy and I knew it was my fault. I was so concerned for him and couldn't bear the thought of him being in pain. Talk about confusion.'

'But why the confusion?' Kate queried. 'If Conrad wants you and you want Conrad where does the confusion come in?' If only it were that easy with her and Guy, she thought. If only Guy cared about her.

Lorraine didn't answer for a minute. She helped herself to more coffee and sugared it heavily. Eventually she raised her eyes to meet Kate's. 'I don't know why I'm telling you all this. It's obvious you have never had a bad hiccup in your love life.

'The reason Conrad and I didn't make it the first time around was because . . . well, he was getting over a messy divorce and was so badly bruised he couldn't cope with his feelings for me and getting into another relationship so soon after the divorce. I'm praying he's got over it all now but terrified of getting hurt again, and all this has been so quick. I mean, how long have we been down here—ten, eleven days?'

'Yes, but you've known Conrad a long time. It's not as if you've just met. You'd buried your feelings because he'd hurt you, but deep down you must know that he really does want to make amends now.'

'Yes, I suppose so,' Lorraine said.

Kate frowned. 'I can't help you make a decision, Lorraine. You have to do that for yourself. But what I don't understand is...' She hesitated because she was really asking this for herself. Lorraine had been hurt, just as she had, but how did you overcome that mistrust? Sophisticated Lorraine was struggling with it, so what hope was there for herself? 'You wanted Guy and I would have thought he was the last man you would be attracted to if you wanted to avoid another broken heart.'

'What do you mean?'

'Well, he has a reputation for being a heartbreaker. I'd say you are safer with a divorced Conrad than you would ever be with Guy... What are you laughing at?'

Lorraine was nearly choking with laughter. She held a napkin to her lips and then dabbed at her eyes. 'Guy has a reputation for being a heartbreaker because he holds himself so aloof that no female in the company has ever got anywhere *near* his heart. Except you, of course,' she added, without malice and with almost a twinkle in her very blue eyes.

Kate's heart thudded. She knew how she felt about Guy but she didn't really know for sure how he felt about her. She couldn't ask, for fear of rejection, but she could try and encourage Lorraine to be a bit more forthcoming; she'd already made a good start. Gossip? She was learning the techniques quick enough.

'You said I'd won, Lorraine. You seem to know more about Guy's feelings than I do,' she admitted, hoping that was enough to tempt Lorraine into revealing more.

'That's probably because I've known him longer than you.' She let out a long sigh. 'You know, I'll always have a soft spot for Guy. Take that as a warning, Kate. If I ever see you giving him a hard time I'll always be there for him.' She stood up, stretched languidly and gazed around the scented courtyard. 'This had a lot to do with my re-awakening over Conrad.'

'What—this courtyard?'

'This old—what do they call it—*finca*?'

'Country house. This was a farm at one time,' Kate volunteered.

'Yes, well, whatever. This place is Guy Latham and you. He knew you would love it and I would hate it. The villa is more me and Conrad. Funny old life, isn't it?' She didn't wait for an answer but clacked her narrow heels over the cobblestones to the arched gate.

Kate called out to her as she tugged at the door. 'This row Guy and Conrad are having; what's it about?' It had been at the back of her mind all the time Lorraine had been purging herself. Perhaps Guy was trying to warn his brother off Lorraine, wanting Lorraine for himself after all. Still she couldn't get the thought of Guy and Lorraine as an item out of her mind.

Lorraine smiled. 'Nothing to do with either of us. Work. Probably why Latham's is so successful. They must have been a terrible handful when they were kids. They score off each other.

'This latest row is about that Roederer deal. The night Conrad was in hospital Guy was in the office all night, faxing round the world trying to get it back in the Latham court; he succeeded too and apparently it's a mega deal. They are rowing about the increased staffing the contract will bring.

Conrad wants to disappear to South America for a long honeymoon. Guy won't let him. I expect they'll sort it out without too much blood being spilt.

'I'll see you later. Perhaps we can get some time to go down to Puerto Banus together and do some shopping.' The door in the wall slammed shut after her.

'Yes, that will be nice,' Kate murmured, and thought it probably would be.

Guy wasn't in the office when Kate arrived. She sat down at her computer and started work as if it were just another working day. But the fact that her heart was thudding wildly inside her breast was confirmation that it actually wasn't just any old working day.

'So what changed your mind?' he asked brittly as he strode into the office half an hour later, obviously surprised to see her sitting at her console.

Slowly she turned to face him, not sure now, knowing she should be sure that he cared for her because she'd had time to pick over the bones of Lorraine's conversation and come up with something to work on. But, of course, faced with him, she wavered, uncertain and vulnerable again but trying to fight it.

'I couldn't let you down,' she murmured, nervously picking at the seam of her skirt. She stopped picking, smoothed the seam determinedly and stood up. 'Especially now you have the Roederers contract and will need extra staff.'

He looked up from his desk, the phone already in his hand, and glared at her. 'How did you know about that?'

She stepped towards him—assertive steps because she was feeling pretty assertive now. She wasn't going to think negatively about anything ever again. She wanted Guy Latham. She trusted him. She loved him, yes, she wanted him, and he must want her because . . . well, because.

'Your brother didn't tell me in some secret corner of the garden, if that's what you're thinking.'

He slammed the phone back into its cradle and glared at her angrily. 'And you can stop that before it goes any further and I really get mad,' he ordered thickly.

'I couldn't resist a last little jab, and it will be the last, Guy. I realise now that all your warnings were—'

'Fanned by jealousy,' he admitted gruffly.

Kate's heart squeezed so tightly with happiness that she thought she would faint. She sat on the edge of his desk and rolled the corner of a piece of paper, staring down at it as she did so. 'As all my accusations about you and Lorraine were fanned by jealousy.'

'So here we are, both awash with jealousy—so what does it mean?' Guy asked.

Kate shrugged without looking at him. 'I guess it means something special.'

'Can't you be more precise?'

She looked up at him then and gave him a small smile. 'Can't you?'

He shook his head slowly and gazed down at a pen he was twiddling between his fingers. 'No, I can't because I can't be sure you won't throw it back in my face.'

'No, Guy Latham.' Kate laughed softly. 'You're not getting away with that.'

He looked up at her and a slow grin started to spread across his face. 'You can't blame me for trying, Kate. Right from the start you held me at arm's length, and when I finally got into your heart you cooled off again. Now, what am I to make of that?'

Because he was grinning at her now she knew she was almost there. She wanted to fling herself at him and tell him how she truly felt, but...

'I've never liked you, Guy,' she started, and then grinned at the appalled look on his face. 'It's true. I hated the way you were, so sharp and arrogant and egotistical. You were everything I despised in a man. And then—' she shrugged helplessly '— something odd happened. I sort of fell in... I sort of...' She flushed hotly. How could she say it when he hadn't? And it was all too soon. They had only just admitted the jealousy they had both felt.

'You fell in love with me,' Guy finished for her.

'No! I mean...'

Guy stood up, slowly edged his chair out of the way, and came round the desk to her. He took her hands and drew her forward so that she slid off the edge of the desk to stand in front of him. He held her hands at her sides, not making any move to take her in his arms.

'Will it help if I tell you I fought falling in love with you too? I thought you were after Conrad and you were so ill suited I thought you must want him for his money. I brought you down here because you were so smart and I needed your working skills. I tested you with the *finca* and began to see the real Kate, and then I was jealous of my own brother and mad at him for using you to get Lorraine back. Then suddenly you were mine and I felt I'd won a battle—but then suddenly I lost it.'

'It would have been all right,' Kate murmured, squeezing his hands tightly, 'if Conrad hadn't broken his silly neck and you hadn't...'

Her heart started thudding. She hadn't trusted him. She had jumped to all the wrong conclusions when she'd found out he had spent the night at the villa with Lorraine. And if Lorraine hadn't told her he'd spent all night in the office trying to haul the Roederer contract back she probably wouldn't be here now.

Kate stepped back from him and slid her hands out from his. She had believed it to be all over but it wasn't. Now she had her own guilt to live with—guilt for not having had faith in him.

'Kate,' he murmured worriedly, 'what are you doing, pulling back from me—?'

'If...if Lorraine hadn't told me about Roederers and how hard you worked that night I'd still believe you and she were—'

Angrily he grasped her and pulled her into his arms, and suddenly his mouth was on hers, punishing her so harshly that she tried to cry out a protest. But then, as the magic seeped under her skin, she knew. The kiss softened, very subtly, and then there was no anger, just deep passion and love and the truth—the truth that Guy loved her deeply and it was she who was putting up the barriers around her heart.

She clung to him—wrapped her arms around him and clung to him as if she would never let him go. 'Oh, I love you, Guy,' she breathed heatedly as their lips parted at last. 'And I'll never give Lorraine reason to think I'm giving you a hard time, and even if I do and she tries to comfort you I'll know that you won't let her. I'll trust you and love you and—'

'And what on earth is going on?' he asked, and lifted her chin to look deep into her misty brown eyes.

Kate giggled. 'Lorraine and I, we had a good old gossip this morning. She told me she'll always have a soft spot for you, but she's going to marry Conrad—and do you know she hated him for hurting her, just as I hated you? And don't you think it's funny how everything has turned out? She ends up with Conrad and I end up with you.'

'Darling, it's how I thought it would all end up from the start,' he told her, and then grinned again. 'No. Correction. It's how I thought it would end up with Lorraine and Conrad. I wanted them to get together again. They need each other. Conrad had a bad marriage and has known some tough times and I've always had his best interests at heart. But you—I've never taken you for granted and I never will. I'm going to work so hard to prove to you that I'm not and never have been what you thought I was.'

'Oh, you don't have to, Guy. I know now I had it all wrong. I'm a rotten judge of character, aren't I? I didn't like Lorraine very much till today and now we are going shopping together. Amazing, isn't it?'

'Amazing,' Guy laughed, and kissed the tip of her nose. 'Sisters-in-law should be good friends.'

Kate gasped, her eyes wide and bright. 'Sisters-in-law?' she cried. 'You mean—'

'Yes, I mean...' He didn't finish—not with words, anyway: his lips completed the sentence. His mouth on hers asked and her lips on his answered and his arms folding her hard against his desirous body made it all complete.

When at last they drew apart they both knew that work would be a hopeless task. Slowly they walked through the scented gardens back to the old guest house, arms wrapped around each other in spite of the oppressive heat. They stopped occasionally, to kiss and whisper words of love, in no hurry because they had the rest of their lives together.

'I love you so very much, Kate,' he told her thickly as they stood by the bed in her bedroom. He slid her blouse from her shoulders and mouthed small kisses across her bare skin. A warm breeze lifted the lace from the window, bringing with it the sweet scent of jasmine.

Kate wanted time to stand still, his words to be in her mind for eternity, and his kisses to be feathering across her body for ever. But then, as she slid her hands under his shirt and splayed her fingers over the magnificence of his hard chest, she wanted so much more.

And she got what she wanted—his sensual caresses, the heat of his body against hers, his kisses exploring and discovering every pulse under her skin. He penetrated her deeply at last, when she was writhing with need, moist and ready for him and gasping words of love. His words of love mingled with hers and they were as one as they moved together, fevered in their need, thrusting themselves higher and higher till they both cried out in the heat of the moment, shuddering against each other, flowing with each other in a heated delirium of sexual love.

And then came the delicious mellowing of mind and spirit and heavy limbs and the soft kisses and murmurings of promises of love for evermore.

'Fantastic tan, Kate,' Ed Hughes complimented her on her first day back in the London office. He perched himself on her console as she cleaned out her desk.

'Not bad, is it, considering I've never worked so hard in my life?'

'*That* bad, was it?'

'Terrible,' Kate confessed with a twinkle in her eye. 'Slave-drivers, the pair of them. Our feet never touched the ground.'

The last week or so they certainly hadn't! She and Guy had hardly seen Lorraine and Conrad—those two in Caesar's palace and she and Guy in the lovely old *finca*. Work had come a very poor second to making love at every opportunity.

'So it was work and more work and no time for...you know what with Lorraine and Guy?'

Kate grinned. 'Now come on, Ed, you know I don't gossip. But, on the other hand, there's always a first time,' she said mysteriously.

Ed leaned forward eagerly. 'Spill,' he urged, eyes glinting.

Kate licked her lips 'You know how you all thought Lorraine felt about Guy? Well, she doesn't any more; in fact she never really did, not properly. It was all Conrad's fault, then he broke his neck in a car accident while I was driving and everyone was absolutely furious. They rushed him to hospital and he's perfectly all right but has to wear this funny collar.

'Anyway, Lorraine realised she was still crazy about Conrad and now they are going to be married. So that means Lorraine will be living in Spain and I get her job. I'm the new marketing manager, but only for about a year because by then I'll probably be pregnant—well, not probably, definitely, I should think, the way things are going. I think that's all.'

She cocked her head to one side as if racking her brains to come up with anything else. 'Oh, yes, I nearly forgot. I get to marry the other Latham, Guy, about next Tuesday, I think—that's if Guy can get the licence in time.'

Ed, who had been listening intently, his mouth gaping open, suddenly burst out laughing—a laugh so loud and raucous that it went right through the open door and into the outer office where all heads shot up and looked their way.

'Pull the other leg, sweetheart, it's got bells on,' Ed teased as he got up and went back to his desk.

'Ting-a-ling,' Kate cried, standing up as Guy walked into her office and swept her into his arms.

'Darling, it's all arranged. Tuesday. And your mother arrives from Italy on Monday. I can't wait to meet her and reassure her that I'm going to make you blissfully happy.' His mouth crushed down on hers and Kate hugged him, lost in his love. 'Had I better tell everyone?' Guy asked when at last he drew his mouth from hers.

Kate happily squeezed her arms around his neck and looked over his shoulder. 'I think they already know.'

As Guy turned around there was a sudden cheer from the outer office, and over that cheer Kate just heard Ed Hughes exclaim, 'Who would have thought it?'

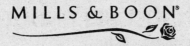

MILLS & BOON®

Next Month's Romances

Each month you can choose from a wide variety of romance with Mills & Boon. Below are the new titles to look out for next month in our two new series Presents and Enchanted.

Presents™

TOO WISE TO WED?	Penny Jordan
GOLD RING OF BETRAYAL	Michelle Reid
THE SECOND MRS ADAMS	Sandra Marton
HONEYMOON FOR THREE	Sandra Field
THE UNEXPECTED FATHER	Kathryn Ross
RYAN'S RULES	Alison Kelly
SUBSTITUTE BRIDE	Angela Devine
THE DOMINANT MALE	Sarah Holland

Enchanted™

BRINGING UP BABIES	Emma Goldrick
FALLING FOR HIM	Debbie Macomber
SECOND-BEST WIFE	Rebecca Winters
THE BABY BATTLE	Shannon Waverly
HIS CINDERELLA BRIDE	Heather Allison
MISLEADING ENGAGEMENT	Marjorie Lewty
A ROYAL ROMANCE	Valerie Parv
LIVING WITH MARC	Jane Donnelly

A SECRET SPLENDOUR
Sandra Brown

After the death of her son, Joey, Arden Gentry
feels a terrible emptiness.

But she has another son, a child she agreed to
give up at birth in a desperate move to save
herself and Joey from an emotional hell.

Now that Joey is gone, Arden is convinced
that the son she's never held could ease her
pain. But she knows that finding him would
resurrect the half-truths, secrets and
unspeakable lies that surround his birth.
Because it means finding the man who
fathered her baby…

"One of fiction's brightest stars!"

Dallas Morning News

MIRA®

SOMEBODY'S BABY
Charlotte Vale Allen

A woman's entire life is turned upside down by
her mother's deathbed confession:
Snow Devane was stolen as an infant and is
someone else's child.

At thirty-one, Snow believes she has
everything—a successful career as a
photographer, an uncomplicated life in
Manhattan, good friends and some necessary
distance from the mother who stifled her with
caring concern.

Now, suddenly, everything has changed—and
there are so many unanswered questions. Who
was this woman she thought she knew? What
drove her to steal another woman's child? What
happened to the woman who, thirty years
before, turned around in a supermarket to find
her baby gone? And, most importantly, who is
Snow Devane?

"A powerful and compelling story."

Rapport

MIRA®

GET 4 BOOKS
AND A MYSTERY GIFT

Return this coupon and we'll send you 4 Mills & Boon Presents™ novels and a mystery gift absolutely FREE! We'll even pay the postage and packing for you.

We're making you this offer to introduce you to the benefits of Reader Service: FREE home delivery of brand-new Mills & Boon Presents novels, at least a month before they are available in the shops, FREE gifts and a monthly Newsletter packed with information.

Accepting these FREE books and gift places you under no obligation to buy, you may cancel at any time, even after receiving just your free shipment. Simply complete the coupon below and send it to:

MILLS & BOON® READER SERVICE, FREEPOST, CROYDON, SURREY, CR9 3WZ.

No stamp needed

Yes, please send me 4 free Mills & Boon Presents novels and a mystery gift. I understand that unless you hear from me, I will receive 6 superb new titles every month for just £2.10* each, postage and packing free. I am under no obligation to purchase any books and I may cancel or suspend my subscription at any time, but the free books and gift will be mine to keep in any case. (I am over 18 years of age)

P6LE

Ms/Mrs/Miss/Mr _____

Address _____

_____

_____ Postcode _____

Offer closes 30th June 1997. We reserve the right to refuse an application. *Prices and terms subject to change without notice. Offer only valid in UK and Ireland and is not available to current subscribers to this series. **Readers in Ireland please write to: P.O. Box 4546, Dublin 24.** Overseas readers please write for details.

mps
MAILING
PREFERENCE
SERVICE

You may be mailed with offers from other reputable companies as a result of this application. Please tick box if you would prefer not to receive such offers. ☐